# BAKER'S DOZEN
## Short Stories from India

# BAKER'S DOZEN

## Short Stories from India

Shoma A. Chatterji

*Rupa & Co*

Copyright © Shoma A. Chatterji 2003

Published 2003 by
Rupa . Co
7/16, Ansari Road, Daryaganj,
New Delhi 110 002

*Sales Centres:*

Allahabad Bangalore Chandigarh Chennai
Dehradun Hyderabad Jaipur Kathmandu
Kolkata Ludhiana Mumbai Pune

Typeset in 11 pts. Revive by
Nikita Overseas Pvt Ltd,
1410 Chiranjiv Tower,
43 Nehru Place
New Delhi 110 019

Printed in India by
Gopsons Papers Ltd.
A-14 Sector 60
Noida 201 301

# Contents

# *Bloodlines*

London, October 3, 2000

My Dear Maa,

Do you realise maa, that this is the first time I am writing a letter to you? A simple thing like a *letter*, maa? And that we've not written a single one to each other? Not *one* single letter? Not *ONE*? Do you remember that in all of my 27 years, this is the first time we have been distanced from each other for more than three days, weekends, to be precise?

It's been a month since we arrived in London. I could not write earlier because apartment-hunting took some time. The cold is too sharp for my asthma. Palash was busy handling details of my temporary work permit, arguing with the customs department regarding the electronic items we'd brought along and so on. Not to talk of arranging for my regular medication.

From faraway London, I can still smell you, I can smell your talcum, your sari, your sweat as you perspire in the small kitchen, strands of sweat-wet hair sticking to your forehead as you season the curry on the gas stove, one end of your red-bordered yellow Tangail jacked up and tucked into your waist. Those are some of the most beautiful moments I have stored forever. Perhaps.

After taking the pot off the stove, you'd ladle a bit of the chicken into one of those small China bowls you brought back from your German trip, toss a spoon into it, and ask me to have a before-taste of my favourite curry. It would be hot-hot-hot, with the smoke rising above in tiny, floating circles. I'd burnt my tongue quite a few times in my hurry to savour the fresh sharpness of the red chillies in it. You'd come running after me, chiding me for being greedy and impatient. At once, I'd break into an impromptu dance in the kitchen, trying to make light of the sharp, burning sensation that hurt so bad on the tip of my tongue. The bowl of curry would wait to cool off. By then, I was too much in pain to before-taste it anymore. It being summer, my asthma would almost disappear. Spicy stuff always worsened my asthma. But you and I often threw caution to the winds and ate what we liked, didn't we maa?

I can feel you through the small silver box of *sindoor* you quietly slipped into my vanity case minutes before I stepped into the departure lounge at Sahara airport. I surprised myself by recognizing it from fractured memories of a broken childhood. It stood out among the sparseness of your toiletries on the dressing table—comb, brush, sticks of Shringar *bindis*, a bottle of *alta,* that tiny phial of *Ma Griffe*, your favourite French perfume, your only concession to the luxury of cosmetics in your drip-dry-life-lived-in-the-singular. I cannot place exactly when the box disappeared from the dressing table along with the bottle of *alta*. Was it *after* Baba left? Or, was it during the long cold war between you? Or, was it much before all this when you realised marriage, for you two at least, had turned into the joke of the Millennium? I dip the silver *sindoor* stick into the box every morning after my head-bath to sprinkle some of the beautiful powder into my hair parting. As if by magic, my face takes on a strange glow. It radiates like sunshine on a rain-washed morning. Or, like a baby flashing a toothless smile the minute momma comes back from work. Why did the same magic fail to work for you, maa? My memories of your lustrous, black tresses are tinged with the widow-like white, *sindoor*-free parting. I have no memory of a red-smeared parting or a *sindoor bindi* adorning your beautiful forehead. Why, maa?

Familiarity breeds contempt they say. Did this happen to you and me, maa? Maybe, it did, because I must confess after all these years that I have always blamed you for the split between Baba and you. The question of rationale was an unknown entity then. Later, as I grew up, there were questions. Questions springing from feelings, not from school lessons. Questions that kept nagging me over time like a fish-bone-trapped-in-the-gullet that has gone away still seems to be stuck where it had been for a few hours. *Khuch-khuch, khuch-khuch* it goes, and keeps pricking you for hours on end. Questions to which I had to seek my own answers. Answers that were erratic, skewed, curved, angular, curvilinear, squarish but never linear or round. Answers which, instead of solving my problems, created more questions, egging me on to dream up my own answers. At such moments, I would part the curtains to gaze out of the window next to my study table and allow my eyes to wander. I would watch pigeons perching themselves on the old and bent banyan tree outside, crows gathered at their regular afternoon conference on the terrace of the house opposite ours, the landlord's gardener treating the soil with manure, while my Math homework sadly waited for attention in the notebook that lay in front. Remember maa, I failed twice in my Math exam the years after your divorce came through? Perhaps, I could have asked you directly, through letters like this. I never had the chance. I always lived with you and those fun-filled weekends with Baba offered neither the time nor the space, nor even the mindset needed to pen serious lines to a MotherYouWouldMeetOnTheMonday anyway.

1. Why don't parents who split up because they cannot get along for whatever reason, cut their kids up into two vertical halves and share these two parts between them?

2. Why do courts, which grant divorce, distribute the kid's week so unfairly between the mother and the father—the mother for the week and the father for the weekend?

3. Why the rigidity of sticking to weekdays for maa and weekends for Baba at all?

4. Why could I not stay over with Baba even when I loved to live with him more than I ever did with you?

5. Why did you take Baba to task that one time I had to overstay through the week because I caught a virus and Baba had to take leave of absence to nurse me back to health?

6. Why did you sternly command me to come home right back the weekend when, just before my 13th birthday, I wished to stay back and look after Baba because the chicken pox that had so kindly spared him when he was little, had caught up with him now?

7. Why did you fire his girlfriend over the phone when you were already divorced? She was really nice you know. She cooked up his favourite brunch on the Sundays she dropped in and stayed back for brunch. Often, the three of us would bundle into Baba's rickety old Fiat and go off to the zoo, or to the Taraporewala Aquarium at Marine Lines, or, to the Museum near Kala Ghoda, or, to any kiddy film that ran in town. I never once saw Babli Auntie after you gave her that tongue-lashing. Never mind that you neatly defended yourself with the cold insularity, convenient anonymity and casual indifference of the telephone. Baba never had a girlfriend again. Though I was fiercely possessive of him, I did feel a bit sad thinking there would be no one to dish up his favourite Sunday brunch any more. By the time I learnt to cook, he was gone.

8. Why were there only the two of us in the same class, Renuka, and myself and just 18 in the whole school from single-parent families? Of which, ten had parents who had divorced and the rest had widowed mothers and fathers? We stuck out like a few sore thumbs in a crowd of beautiful, graceful, lovely, soft hands with thumbs all in the right place. We often caught our teachers whisper to each other as they looked at

Renuka and me in turns. Renuka would establish eye contact with me in silent conspiracy, and in complete agreement, we understood what they were whispering about—the two of us and about our parents—divorced. When I failed my Math exam the first time, I was only eight. Instead of scolding me roundly and asking me to do better, Miss Parameswaran clucked her tongue in sympathy, shook her head this way and that, and patted me softly on my head. I feel the anger and the bitterness rise in me all over again as I re-live the experience now, in writing. I was really angry.

9. Why make something special out of a child's failure and blame it on the parents' divorce for God's sake? As if children from families where the parents are together, are all Einsteins and Isaac Newtons and Wordsworths in-the-making? As if their parents don't ever fight or quarrel or abuse each other for whatever reason?

10. Why did you have to spoil all the fun of you and I living together by throwing your 'sacrifice' bit on my face all the time? Pushing it like a bitter pill down my throat each time I shared with you some fun thing I had done with Baba that weekend? My asthma pills were bearable when compared to the pills of your oblique hints that hurt, and hurt bad. "I kept myself aloof from men who appeared interested because you might not have liked it, Bula," you would say so often that I began to anticipate precisely when, how and in what circumstances you would say it again. "I have given up my friends and my social circle because I have to play

single parent to you," was another boring phrase you abused with overuse. It is not your sacrifice maa. It never was. If you could not deal with Baba and he with you, it was your problem. The sacrifice is all mine. I was *forced* to give up the normal joy of living with both parents under the same roof. You *chose* to live apart from each other. The 'choice', let me remind you, was never mine. My entire life was sucked into the hateful routine of a split week—Mondays through Fridays with you and weekends with Baba. All this, without break unless something catastrophic had to happen to one of you. Like Baba's jaundice and your accident. And Di'maa's death. I have never had the good fortune of watching my parents exchange messages through glances thrown at each other in a crowded room. What is 'normal' for most children, has to be labelled 'good fortune' in my case. Why, maa?

Questions like these, and many more, dogged my growing years right till I was old enough to accept that my life was a bit skewed and would remain that way till I got married and had my own family. It was like a notebook with the borders of each page torn away any which way, eaten away by rats - rough, uneven, ugly. You cannot throw it away because the glossy cover fools you and the pages are all blank and new and fresh. Nor can you use it because not a single leaf in the notebook is whole. The only question I was scared to ask myself was the most precious and the most fiercely guarded one—*why did you two have to part at all, maa?* It does not matter anymore. It will not bring back and set right all those years of pining for one parent while living with the other, will it? Does this happen to all children of divorced parents forced to live with one parent and have the other one for holidays and weekends only? Does it, maa?

I asked Renuka once. Her story was sadder than mine was. I knew she had a twin brother, Rajeev, but I did not know that the court had decided to separate the children along with their parents—something the two tiny tots—they were five then and had just begun nursery—could not even begin to understand. Rajeev would live with their father and Renuka with the mother. As if separating twins at five was not enough, their father lived in Bangalore and the mother, in Mumbai! What sort of justice was this, maa? They'd meet for the holidays. These too, were neatly broken up into watertight compartments. In summer, the twins would be with their mother and Christmas was to be spent with the father.

"It was so confusing and painful that both of us began to dread the holidays by the time we reached the higher classes," Renuka told me. "Because, in the summer holidays, mummy would desperately try to make up for not having 'mothered' Rajeev. She'd overfeed him, overprotect him so much that he would begin to feel throttled and I, neglected. She'd beat me up during every tiff between Rajeev and me and kiss him all over his face which he did not like one bit. During Christmas, it was the opposite. Daddy would try to compensate for the days he had missed his only daughter. He would shower me with so many ice-creams that I'd invariably fall sick with a sore throat. He'd load me with presents I did not really need. Till my play-cupboard spilled over with teddy bears and dolls and toy trains. He'd give Rajeev a tongue-lashing for no reason whatsoever, mainly in my presence. Maybe he felt, with his own skewed logic, that it would make me happy. But I felt Rajeev's pain soak into me as if, it was my own. I blamed both Mum and Dad for decimating whatever little happiness we could have rescued from the debris of our fractured lives by remaining together. We wanted to share the pain of living out a divided loyalty we did not believe in. Just to make both parents angry with the two of us, we hatched a plan. We decided that Rajeev would take up cigarettes, a deadly habit Daddy abhorred, and I would be casual about my homework to bring down my high grades. True to our promise, Rajeev turned into a heavy smoker right through his eighth standard till he finished school. All the generous pocket money Dad allowed him was spent away on Lady Nicotine. My grades began to fall steadily. My class teacher advised Mummy to go in for counselling. We kept tabs on each other through long-distance telephone calls. The deed was done. But at the end of it all, strange though this may sound, this did not make us feel vindicated at all. We felt sad, empty, drained.

"Rajeev was packed off to the IIT for his engineering—he managed to excel in studies. I really don't know how. But he remains an obsessive smoker to this day. I turned over a new leaf after the counselling. 'It is stupid, you know, to take your anger against your parents out on your studies,' said Deepa Pundlik, my counsellor, when she realised soon after the sessions began, that my school grades were bad because I *wanted* them to be bad. "She is trying to draw your attention to herself," said Pundlik to Mummy. I saw her face begin to crumble at once into a cry. She let off her pent up anger on me when we went home. "How *could* you?" she repeated, *ad infinitum*, a phrase that was an inseparable part of her limited vocabulary. Since the divorce, I was so used to her irrational outbursts that I shut off my senses to her bouts of anger and sunk myself into the living room sofa with the remote in my hand."

Renuka's account of her childhood made my own seem much lighter and rosier in comparison. It took more than a week for her to throw up small details of her fragmented life. We sat on the wide parapet outside the school building at Dadar Hindu Colony, after school hours, throwing absent-minded glances at passers-by who glanced back at us strangely and walked away. The fenced off tennis court behind offered strange background support to our tête-à-têtes, the rhythmic, well-timed plop-plop-plop of the tennis ball moving back and forth in court subtly hinting at two very different world spaces existing right beside each other. So close, yet so very far, like you and Baba were, even when the three of us—(two-and-a-quarter rather, because I was seven when you split) lived together at our Dadar flat. Some days, I'd take Renuka to one of the booths at the Udipi place nearby. Over plates of idli-chutney downed with steaming hot filter coffee drunk from small stainless steel glasses placed in small stainless steel pots, the two of us would rub a bit of our pains into each other, keeping the rest for ourselves. "No one ever asked me what my life is like," she said. "I'm glad you gave me the chance," she added, planting a sudden kiss on my cheek, taking me completely by surprise. Not used to physical signs of affection, I shied away from all kinds of human touch. Besides, "it is bad for your asthma" you'd warned me time and again. One of the few commands of yours I did not bother to defy.

After Renuka and I joined the same college, we drifted apart, because Renuka evolved into an incorrigible shirt-chaser, picking and dropping one boyfriend after another and cutting classes like a chronic bunker. She acquired the label of an outrageous flirt. But I knew and understood that she was looking for a boy who would perhaps replace the emotional vacuum created by her enforced separation from Rajeev, her twin, "the other half of myself." We have not been in touch since college. Pain breeds pain, and this is why one sad person cannot be friends with another sad one. That is one more emotional struggle children of schizophrenic families must go through—alienation from society and distancing from peers. But how would you know all this maa? Di'maa and Dadu, as you said so yourself and I saw with my little-girl eyes, happily shared the bonding of married togetherness for forty long years, till Di'maa died of cancer and Dadu faithfully followed a year later.

Why am I purging myself of past pains after 20 years maa? Why do I pick you for all the purging? Why not Baba, you must be thinking. I have written to Baba, maa, because I was distanced from him most of the time. Distance, though it sounds contradictory, has the merit of allowing one to air one's feelings through letters, you know. There weren't any faxes or e-mails then, where you have to cut out the emotion to save on the telephone bill and make your message feel, look and sound like a truncated version of a small-boy-who-is-weak-in-English's homework. *"Hi Baba, Thank u for the mail. Got ur pix. Will wait for ur rep. Am missing u. Luv. Bi."* As a literature student, it gives me the jitters to read this kind of stuff. Palash laughs and calls me old-fashioned and I tell him right back, "if speaking and writing perfectly understandable English is being old-fashioned then well, so be it. I *am* one."

When you took me away to Di'maa's for the summer holidays, I had all the chance in the world to write to Baba, remember? They were short, very short notes, about what I had done that day in Pune, or, re-living in writing, one of our fun weekends together. The neem tree in granny's garden blew a strange sort of bitter-moist breeze on a windy day with the coming of the first showers. My mind seemed to develop a hole in it. It somehow felt empty. Because Baba was not there with us. How can emptiness feel 'heavy'? It did, believe me. He wrote back sometimes, not always, because we were both sure that you'd tear his letters up before they reached my hands, my eyes, my heart. Di'maa had instructed Bhola Dada to give them to me in secret, whenever he opened the letter box first. I left them behind in Pune. I felt I was leaving behind a part of Baba behind, so that I could feel him through those letters whenever I came back for holidays to re-read them. To re-live the experience and feel a little slice of Baba by my side. Always.

Life is full of the strangest contradictions one does not find a parallel to, in literature or in films. I was once asked to make a presentation at a literary seminar on *Marriage Schisms in Contemporary Indo-Anglian Fiction by Women Writers*, remember maa? The three writers I chose were Nayantara Saigal, Anita Desai and Shashi Deshpande. The research was so drab and dry that along the way, I forgot I myself was a child of divorce. I had chosen the topic in the first place precisely because I was one. The research proved how distanced real life is from its reflection, interpretation, transliteration in writing. You encapsulate a fragmented, once-intimate relationship by breaking it into analysis and research. And in so doing, you strip it off all credibility, of the emotional trauma that forms part of the split, the social re-definition of relationships the children have to cope with, against their will. I spoke about the fluency of their language, the beauty of their style. I commented on the way they used metaphor, imagery, simile to draw upon real life situations. I opined on their choice of time and setting. I quoted their descriptions of Nature and Character and commended their insight into people and relationships.

Though my paper was roundly praised for its 'insightful analysis' from my learned colleagues, I knew it was as dry as a tree in a Delhi winter, stripped of leaves and flowers, of juice and life, standing alone and forlorn, silhouetted against the winter sky, waiting for a touch of spring to bring back to it the lush velvety green of fresh foliage, the fragrance and colours of flowers and the smell of the fresh earth underneath. It waited for children to come and play around it, pluck flowers off its green-lined branches, pick some leaves off the ground. My paper could not put into words, even a moment of the emotional trauma, of the pain the different members—parents, the couple in question, and their children, agonisingly journeyed through. My paper was a clinical dissection of a literary piece—a post-mortem on a live 'body' of literary creation which robbed the stories of the life they palpably vibrated with, when read in the original. Strangely however, through the time I worked on the paper, the constant pain of living out a drawn-and-quartered life, was forgotten.

This letter to you is to tell you how sorely I missed Baba every single minute I lived away from him, and *with* you. I know how ungrateful that sounds, how absolutely self-centred, heartless and brutal. But this is the truth, maa and it is time we buried those lies we shared once for all. I love you maa, but can I help it if I love Baba more? Each time he asked me to get into his car to drop me back 'home' I felt a heart-wrenching pain inside me. I felt the blade of a knife enter my stomach and turn and twist inside, taking my insides out to litter them all about the pavement in front of Baba's apartment. I saw myself pick them up, gather them together and put them back into my tummy. I remember weeping inconsolably in the beginning. Later, I taught myself to drink in my tears, because I knew it would make him sadder to see me cry.

Nor did I wish to let on to you that I hated to come back. But your sensitive maternal antenna was always up. Every Monday morning, as you opened the door to me, you'd ask me why my eyes were so red-rimmed and swollen. Why I wasn't smiling. Why I had forgotten to comb my hair, or knot the tie of my uniform just so. Why my socks were smelling and my shoes remained unpolished. Did you guess the right answers to your questions maa? Or did you, like always, force yourself to turn your back to them and concentrate on my school tiffin? Or begin to iron my salwar-kurta that did not need ironing? Did you ponder over the same questions at work in your office? Forgetting to update your files, attend to the latest correspondence? I'd notice your absent-mindedness, your anxiety, your nervous tics break up into longish lines on your smooth face every Monday and Friday, the days I returned from and went to stay with Baba, for the weekend.

Baba remarried and migrated to the States, after I had just celebrated my 17th birthday with my college friends. He wrote me a letter telling me about it. This time, you gave me the letter. You probably wanted to escape the responsibility of giving me the news yourself. I had known it was coming. Baba never kept secrets from me. At the time, I felt happy thinking Baba would not have to live alone anymore. That he would not drink as much as he had lately begun to. But his decision to migrate was the biggest shock of my life. I locked myself up in my small room and refused to answer your loud banging on the door. I shut my ears to your desperate calls of 'Bula, Bula, please open the door, please. Is it my fault? What have I done? Please Bula' you went on and on, for hours at stretch, till Sulekha, the maid, came and dragged you away. By then, your cries had toned down to sad, whimpering sounds. So drowned was I in my obsession with self-pity, that it did not move me at all. "She'll come out Didi, don't push her and she will" said Sulekha, wizened beyond her twenty-odd years.

I picked at my food for weeks together, kept staring at the ceiling those nights when sleep played truant, refused to meet friends, or answer the telephone, and switched off the television even while you were pretending to watch it. This repatterning of my life—that I would not have to go away on weekends anymore—ought to have made me happy. It didn't. The shock of his having left without bidding me goodbye ("there was no time my pet and I had to rush" he'd scribbled in a hurried hand) was too much for a seventeen-year-old-only-child-of-divorced-parents to handle. It's been ten years now and the hurt seems to have healed. It has at least taken care of my asthmatic attacks. They are much less now than they used to be when I had to drag my unwilling feet back to you each Monday morning before the schoolbus arrived. At least, I don't have to live a lie every single minute of my life anymore.

It is the middle of October and the London chill is just beginning to make itself felt. We live in a brownstone as paying guests of a Sindhi family in Wembley. It has so many Gujaratis that you might begin to doubt whether you were in London at all. The streets are lined with shops selling Indian stuff from South Indian dosas to *Screen* and *Filmfare* to huge picture postcards of Madhuri Dixit and Amitabh Bachchan. A woman in a sari draped Gujarati style, is as common a sight as it is on the streets of Mumbai. The chill is so infectious that it seems to have entered into my system, cooling off my emotions in some mysterious way. The Sindhi couple brought me a cough syrup the other day. How would they know that the cold was within me? That the physical symptoms of a cold fever were just because of the climatic change I was facing? The sudden drop in the temperature worsened my asthma. Palash has had to take me to the doctor. But, I know and he does not, that the greater chill is inside me, not outside.

The trees have begun to shed their leaves now that Autumn is at an end. The chill has helped me place my life in perspective, infusing my thoughts with an objectivity I did not have when I lived in India, with you. Sometimes, at night, the chill seems to have entered my heart, sending all feelings into deep freeze. Unlike frozen food taken out of the refrigerator, it does not seem to thaw. Our Gujarati neighbours who run an Indian grocery nearby came to make friends. Palash was thrilled but I was cool, almost frosty in my response, in keeping with the London weather that evening. Was I afraid of questions about my past? Maybe I was, maybe, I wasn't. The most important thing for me at the moment was to write this letter to you and to purge myself of my past. Completely. To put it behind me. Forever.

This letter is a reflection of my emptiness, my vacuum, my emotional chasm of the past 20 years. It is an expression of feelings left unsaid because we were too close and too scared to say things upfront that would hurt each other. We were too close to write letters to. Yet, emotionally, too distanced to sit down and have a mother-daughter showdown. Or, a 'sisterly discussion' if you want it put that way. Your divorce came through when I was seven, remember, maa? Would you believe this if I tell you that Palash glimpsed his first rainbow at that age? That, without knowing Wordsworth at all then, had written a poem about it to show it to his teacher? That the teacher had asked him to read it out to the whole class?

I have mellowed far beyond my 27 years. Palash is a good husband. I have decided to place all my emotional investments into seeing that our children, when we have them, will not suffer the loneliness and the social alienation and the pain I did. So has Palash. I am teaching myself to erase the memories of those lovely weekends with Baba because they are painful to recall in retrospect. I must confess that I did write to Baba in the US to begin with. They've got a little boy now. They've sent me pictures of Robin. I pray that this little half-brother of mine does not have to go through the agony I did. But I have stopped writing letters to Baba. It does not seem to mean anything, either way.

I know this sounds clichéd and melodramatic. But I really want to start life afresh. With this letter, maa, I am pressing the DELETE key on the keyboard of the computer of my relationships. Never mind how close they are. I am waiting for the command to take effect. That command called SAVE does not exist in my CPU, believe me. The MEMORY is corrupted by that emotional virus called pain. I realised long ago that the only key that was burdened with overuse—or would abuse be a better word—in your computer, also Baba's, was ESCAPE. If this sounds like a cruel betrayal, read this letter all over again from start to finish. And again. It will perhaps help ease your pain. Perhaps, make you realise who was the one betrayed - was it you, was it Baba, were it you two together, or was it me? Did I say this is my first letter to you? Well, sorry, maa, but this is also my last. Bloodlines do not really matter after all, do they maa?

Love and fare-well,

Yours,
Bula.


*When Sharmila finished reading the letter, she read it twice again. Did it ease her pain like Bula said it would? She did not know yet. She surprised herself as she saw that her eyes remained dry. Absolutely, completely dry. Throughout the long epistle, Bula used a capital 'B' while referring to Baba,* her form of address for her father. But for maa she spelt the 'm' in small case. This itself gave away her own importance in Bula's life. Yet, there were no tears. Life had sucked her tears dry. Through her growing up years, Bula hardly hid the fact that she was closer to her father Indra, than to herself. Sharmila accepted this with grace after the first shock of discovery was over. What shocked her was this new knowledge about Bula having hated to live with her all along. That she regretted every minute of sharing the same roof with her. She tried to feel Bula through the stationery she had penned the letter on. Bula had used recycled paper to pen the letter. Environment-friendly? Yes. Mother-friendly? No. Sharmila smiled a caustic smile as she absent-mindedly folded the letter into four neat little rectangles and slipping it back into the envelope it came in, placed it on the bedside table, next to the framed photograph of Bula and Indra with their arms wrapped around each other, laughing into the camera. She walked up to the window facing the banyan tree outside, and sighed at the irony hidden between the lines of the letter like those hidden crooks and corners between the branches of this doddering old tree. An irony Bula was a part of but did not know about.

The last sentence of Bula's letter kept haunting her all day. It taunted her, teased her, played hide-and-seek with her thoughts, making her wake up to the black comedy of their lives after many years. "Bloodlines do not really matter after all, do they maa?" Bula had asked. Rhetorically, not expecting an answer because the letter did not carry Bula's London address. How easy it was for Bula to trap a 27-year-old mother-daughter relationship within the environment-friendly pages of a letter penned once in all those years from faraway London. And to end it with that. Like a part of your anatomy being cut off for no reason. When nothing was wrong with it. But, thought Sharmila to herself—relationships too turn gangrenous, don't they? Perhaps, Bula understood this and she did not. Bula's language, like always, was strong, confident, assertive–leaving no trace of doubt that she would live up to her promise to herself–this would be her last letter as well.

Over the first seven-and-odd years that she and Indra led a 'normal' family life, Indra, Sharmila noticed, loved the little girl to distraction. And the little girl they named Bula after Indra's dead sister, loved him right back–smothering him with kisses with her tiny mouth, caressing him with her podgy fingers, wrapping her little hand around his finger as she tottered through her first steps, flashing him magic toothless smiles the minute he stepped inside the door as he came back from work, throwing up all over his business-suit a minute before he was to walk out to an important business meeting. She scribbled all her drawing books with her childish, sketches of a matchstick-father bouncing his matchstick—'baby' high up in the air.

Over time, as the little girl grew into an attractive teenager, she began to resemble Indra strongly. Some of these magic moments were captured for posterity in the freezes of their 'family' album, one of the few things Bula had forgotten to take along. Sharmila often thumbed through its dog-eared pages these days, trying to fill in the empty spaces of her jigsaw-puzzle life with imaginary pictures of what-might-have-been had Indra and she not fallen apart somewhere along the way. Most of the photographs framed Indra and Bula together, *with Sharmila missing because she was the one handling the camera. She was literally offered a point-of-view perspective of the father-daughter intimacy through the lens of the Pentax. The zoom closed in on the father-daughter pair. But she herself remained distanced. She realised that inspite of desperately trying to belong, they had kept her outside the parameters of the frame. Only a few photographs captured Sharmila in them. One was Sharmila with Indra as a young bride. And another was on Bula's first birthday, showing Bula on Sharmila's lap as Indra cut the cake. There was one of hers with Bula in her fancy dress at the school gala. But the glitter of the colourful costume was diluted by the glum expression on Bula's face, looking directly into the camera. The painted scene on canvas in the background gave away the plasticity of the studio ambience.*

*"Bloodlines do not really matter after all, do they maa?" Bula wrote. "You are right, my dear, they don't" said Sharmila to herself. She quietly walked up to the wardrobe of her bedroom. She opened it with the right key from the bunch of keys that always hung from her slender waist, announcing her movements with its musical jingling, poking holes into the sad silence of the flat. Sharmila took out the album of a 'family' that never was, yet had grown, through love. "Hate, not love," she reminded herself. Moving to her bed, slowly, very slowly, she rested her tired head on the headstand. She leafed through the pages of the album, taking in one sepia-tinted, grainy photograph after another, in deliberate slow motion. The protective tissue paper that ran between the thick pages made soft, shuffling noises. "Good, that you will never learn the truth" said Sharmila to an absent Bula, faraway in*

London. She ran her fingers softly over a picture of four-year-old Bula bawling away in her school uniform, schoolbag slung over one shoulder with water bottle in tow, holding Indra's hand. Her skin tingled as she thought she could feel Bula through the old, grainy, sepia-tinted photograph.

Bula would never know that Indra was not her father. When Indra married Sharmila, she was already two months pregnant. It wasn't Indra. Who the father was, did not really matter. Not then. Not now. The colours in Sharmila's memory had faded, blurred into anonymity, like lovely pastel shades on a water colour painting exposed to sunlight fading away with time. Nor did Indra know that Bula was not sired by him.

Then the tears came, without warning, streaming down her cheeks, hollowed by the diabetic diet she was under. A single tear-drop fell on the photograph. Sharmila wiped it away with the end of her sari, smiling through her tears. Almost hoping it would wipe away the tear off Bula's bawling face. "On second thoughts, bloodlines do matter Bula, but neither you, nor Indra have the emotional depth to realise it" she said, more to herself than to a faraway Bula. "Do you realise Bula that this is the first time I am reading a letter written by you to me, and perhaps, reading into your mind as well? A mind, I now realise, I felt I was confident about but did not really know at all? Yet. Bloodlines do matter. And because they do, I, at a world-weary 55, sit in this empty house all alone, often talking to the walls around me, with the television switched on to any channel just to make the sound disguise the silence of the apartment. Trying to share my lonely hours with your photographs in this album again and again and again, till I know them by heart, backwards to front and back.

*Bloodlines do matter. If they didn't, I would have flown to faraway US in place of your father with a brand new husband. Perhaps, a new child in my life. Bloodlines, like it or not, do run thicker than water. Alongwith my sorrow and my loneliness, stripped into ribbons of pain by the razor-sharp edge of your knife-like letter, I cannot help but feel a bit of pity for you Bula. Perhaps, also for Indra, for living in a fool's paradise and not even knowing it."*

# Diamonds Are Forever

When I look at all the jewellery nicely laid out on our large double-bed, I feel like throwing up. Yes, that's true. You might wonder why. And how. Because women love jewellery, don't they? I did too. When I got married, I was awe-struck by all the jewellery Amar's family showered on me. I would deck myself up every evening on the dot of four, dressed to the tee, rich sari, matching blouse with the sleeves coming down to my elbows, and of course, jewels. Jewels that matched my outfit. Corals for an outfit dominated by orange. Rubies to go with a ruby-red sari, emeralds for green, *lapiz lazuli* for blue, and so on. Jaipuri *jadau, minakari* from Hyderabad, *navratan* from Tribhuvandas Bhimji Jhaveri in Bombay, diamonds from Surat and Belgium and delicately crafted gold from the *karigars* of Calcutta at P.C. Chandra's, were enough to fill a room.

But all the jewels paled next to the diamonds. It scares me when I try to measure their weight in money terms, they are so many—in number, quality, shape and colour. Amar has enlarged the collection by adding in his own, every year. The 'neela', that famous diamond with a blue tint shaped into a complete set of bangles, necklace, ear-rings and ring he presented to me on our fifth wedding anniversary. Glittering, shimmering, gleaming in the darkest of rooms, specially ordered from some famous Surat diamond-setter whose name I do not remember. Amar gently teaches me the finer points of how to pick out a genuine diamond from a fake. "A diamond is known by its four 'C's," he says. Cut, Carat, Clarity and …I forget what the last one is. I don't care. I have stopped listening to his long epistles on jewellery and everything that goes with it. Period. I am a bad student of the science of recognising stones, or the beauty of diamonds for that matter. I am no longer interested in them.

"But diamonds are good for your depression, Jhumpa," says Amar's family astrologer, also a birth-stones specialist, Debkanto Bhattacharjee. Bhattacharjee's father was the family astrologer before him and his grandfather before that. For my depression, I am taken to the astrologer, not the doctor. This heredity thing, 'ancestry' as they like to call it, is a baggage Amar's family loves to carry through generations. For them, it is not 'baggage', though, it is a sign of 'class' and 'aristocracy'. Diamonds are an integral part of it. Amar is crazy about having me wear this four-carat diamond solitaire, centred on a thick gold band that holds the finger so tight that I can never take it off. It is a rare piece Amar's great-grandfather acquired from a Belgian collector of antique jewellery who came down to India on invitation by the then-Viceroy. I've forgotten his name though Amar has told me the story so many times that by now I should have got it by heart back to front. He sold a house to buy it for Amar's great-grandmother. The lucky woman, 'lucky' according me, did not have to wear it for long. She died at childbirth–her fourteenth in as many years–three months later. Strange that the family did not consider it 'unlucky' that the wearer of the solitaire died so soon after she began to wear it. Was she expendable by then? I do not know. Nearly a century later, I have no way of finding out.

My only introduction to Srimati Urmila Bala Devi is through the large oil portrait of the lady hanging on the staircase-landing of the ancestral family's big house at Bhawanipur. Who the painter used to model the portrait on, I do not know. Because in those days, a woman from aristocratic families like his great-grandmother was from, remained in *purdah*. She, like those others, lived in the *andar mahal*–the inner house and never appeared in the presence of males who were not 'family'. The diamonds Urmila Bala wore, in the portrait, were painted on so realistically that they glitter in the darkness of the ill-lit landing of the staircase. Why the landing, I ask myself. As if she is still relegated to an existence in limbo, hanging somewhere between the upper floors and the ground floor, like she was, while she lived in the house, a hundred years ago. The colours on the portrait have faded with time, unevenly, turning her stiff smile into an ugly grimace, yet keeping the diamonds untouched. Time has a cruel way of turning things around to mean exactly the opposite of what they were originally supposed to mean. Or, was it a grimace to begin with and has remained so, many years later? Though I know that it brought ill luck to its first wearer, I cannot dream of taking the ring off, ever. If I do, I know Amar will have a nervous breakdown—he is paranoid about this ring. For my part, I feel this ring is the first concrete metaphor of my imprisonment within marriage to Amar. I call it 'imprisonment,' or a kind of 'shackling' if you want it put that way. Many women would have loved to be in my shoes, I know. I too was overwhelmed by the sheer volume of the jewellery when I got married. After all, I was only 21, the last of five daughters my mother had had to deliver, waiting for the precious male heir to make an appearance. He did, when I was two years old. And at last, my mother was liberated from the burden of perennial pregnancy. Not for long however. Because she died when Ratan, our only brother, was eight. My father married again, re-writing the story of our childhood enriched by a step-mother who broke every fairy-tale stereotype of the ugly step-mother. She underscored her one-ness with us by refusing to mother a child of her own. She achieved all this without the aid of jewellery, or diamonds.

When I looked at the bridal trousseau that arrived from the groom's family on the third day of our wedding, I was speechless. I had never seen so much jewellery in my whole life. This was much more than all the gold and precious stones my father and step-mother gave away to my four older sisters when they were married. In comparison, what my parents gave me, which was not very modest either, was an embarrassment. Amar gently persuaded me to keep them safely stored in the new safe deposit locker we jointly opened at the Jodhpur Park branch of his bank. He kept the locker key with him though, because he would be the one to control the locker. It was not the done thing in his family for the *bahu* to visit the bank and take out her jewellery herself. At 21, it was a lovely feeling to be showered with so much protectiveness, with exquisite jewellery, with diamond-studded ornaments of all hue and colour. Feelings, rather. Many kinds of feelings. Good and happy feelings. Feelings with colour and music and smell. Feelings you could almost touch. Feelings that were fragrant and could be heard, read, understood, felt. Feelings that glittered and shone and shimmered in the dark, like my diamonds.

For any invitation, my dear mother-in-law, when she was alive, would select my wardrobe for me, aided and abetted by her favourite son Amar. "Wear the turquoise *minakari* set tonight. It goes well with the turquoise Benarasi," Amar would add. Amar took up where his mother left off, after she passed away. He carries on with it till this day, 25 years since we were married and two days since Reema, our only child, celebrated her first wedding anniversary. By the time Reema got married, I had no idea what my wardrobe looked like. It was Amar who looked after it, cleaned it, dotted it with mothballs and kept tiny balls of perfumed cotton within the sari folds. He maintained all records of my jewellery, blouses, saris, adding to the list every year for Durga Pooja or Diwali or any family wedding, birthday, what-have-you. He needed no excuse to buy me an expensive sari or a new piece of jewellery, diamonds mostly. He took them for periodical polishing at the family jeweller's. "Diamond jewellery will sparkle if cleaned with a few drops of whisky or gin," he says and squats on the floor of our bedroom to translate word into action. He buys whisky and gin exclusively for my diamonds because he is a teetotaller himself. He has the time and the energy to do all this because his accountancy practice never really picked up. Yet, money does not seem to be a problem because Amar's father left a huge estate behind. The earnings from rented premises all over the city are more than enough for running an exorbitantly expensive household. This is split among the three brothers and their families. What really helps in our case—mine, Amar's and Reema's, when we chose to become a nuclear family, now that I look back, is my government job that brings home a neat five-figure sum every month. The *bahu* who does not have the sanction of going to the locker to take out her jewels, is permitted to hold on to a nine-to-five job in the accounts office of the state government. "We know to keep up with the times, we are progressive," say Amar and his sisters and brothers. So what if this 'progressiveness' is tainted with that slight dose of regression? "No" for the locker, "Yes" for the high-salaried government job. Amar and his people have conveniently coined their own definition of 'progress' by re-defining it on their own terms through funny little "Yes's" and "No's" to the most mundane questions of life.

This evening, we are celebrating Reema's first wedding anniversary, with a party from our side. It is our anniversary gift to Reema and her husband Rohit. Tomorrow, they leave for Bombay, where they have been living since they married last year. In keeping with his nature, Amar has bought me a heavy, blue-bordered Tanchoi saree in white with all-over *zardozi* embroidery done in silver thread. The sari had a matching blouse-piece and like he does every time, Amar took a sample blouse from my collection to the tailor down the street and got it tailored to be ready today. He does not like me to visit the tailor. "Don't strain your gout," he says. And I wonder when I had gout. He also went to the bank locker this morning to fetch the latest diamond set. A beautiful piece set in platinum from the De Beers house. It has the first letter of my name "J" crafted out to form the pendant in the long platinum 'disco' chain. The letter is repeated on the graceful bracelet, the brilliant ear-studs and the ring. I hate it but I keep my feelings to myself. Now I have only sad feelings. Feelings that are dark and black and stinking and make me cringe to their touch. Feelings sans colour and fragrance and happy memories.

When we were younger, he stopped me from visiting the tailor with the excuse that I was tired after a heavy day at the office. I was thrilled to discover that my parents had found the most considerate, caring and loving of husbands for me. My friends, while I had them, were jealous. I have few friends left. Most of them soon warmed up to Amar's strong negative vibes towards them when they dropped in. The ones that are still around, mostly within the office and the rest through telephonic contact, envy me because I have a husband like Amar. I am totally dependent on him for my shoes, my sandals, my cosmetics, my dress, my jewellery, my diamonds. Strange that I have unwittingly separated the diamonds from the rest of my jewellery. I always speak of them as having an existence apart. Amar also takes care of my bank account, my income tax returns, and the car, earmarked just to drop me at my office and bring me back. Reema, I suspect, is a wee bit jealous because Rohit does not believe in handing it all out to her on a golden platter like Amar does. When she was with us, she would often chide her father for spoon-feeding me, a woman who could hold down an excellent government job for more than two decades. A woman who held two postgraduate degrees of no mean merit from Calcutta University. They shared secret jokes between them. I did not care to find out what their secret was. The bonding between them was stronger than the bonding I had with Reema. My emotions, whatever little of them are left, have been chipped off me, slowly and surely, turning me into a mechanical clothes-peg, a home-made mannequin without heart or soul, a model for exquisite jewellery and a walking showcase for priceless diamonds with their three C's–I forget the fourth–cut, carat, clarity.

As I pick the items of the De Beers set one by one and put them on, the diamond-encrusted pendant shaped to a 'J', the bright ear-studs repeating the 'J', the 'J'-shaped centre on the platinum ring on my finger, the exquisitely crafted bracelet with the 'J', Amar slips in through the half-closed door to hand me the ironed sari, the matching petticoat, blouse and bra. I hate it all. In all these years, I have never once worn a sari of my own choosing. I have never been permitted to step out of the home sans a single piece of jewellery. I have learnt to ignore the stares of people at cinema halls, frozen on the diamonds I wear to watch a simple movie at the theatre round the corner. I ignore the sarcasm generously handed out by my office colleagues. I have forgotten what I look like without jewellery. When I look at myself in the privacy of the bathroom mirror, it is the heavy, all-time gold necklace round my neck, the pearl studs in my ears that catch my eye first. The face comes second. I don't like to look at it for long, because it appears too pale and colourless to me, in contrast with the brilliance of the gold and the quiet dignity of the pearls. My nose disappears behind the brilliant diamond stud I wear on the left nostril. My weak chin appears weaker above the heavy necklace stringed with gold coins from a bygone era. The only feature I can look at are my eyes—they sparkle in the dark, like tiny diamond stones, the shine drawn from unshed tears of 25 years. I do not wish for that sparkle to disappear—it is the only sparkle that keeps reminding me of myself, reassuring me with the existentialist philosophy that says—"I exist, therefore I am". So, I keep them in control, unshed, unknown, my very own.

All my blouses for the 25 years of my life with Amar have been high-necked and elbow-length. I do not know what wearing a maxi or a nightie feels like because Amar won't hear of it. "Your lovely figure will be distorted out of shape with a maxi or a nightie. All it needs are the graceful folds of the Indian sari," he says, as he plants a loving peck on my cheek. I look with envy at my female colleagues in office, portly and forty-ish, strolling in lazily in a casual salwar-kurta. I have never been allowed to wear black, my favourite colour, because "it is the colour of mourning and of death. It does not suit the colour of your skin," says Amar. At 46, does the colour of the skin really matter? Do flashy clothes suit me at an age when my waistline cannot be framed within the rectangle of my life-size mirror? Why should I put on a glossy red lipstick when the beiges and the soft browns suit me better? Why should I, like today's teenagers, wear diamonds with the first letter of my name encrusted in them? But Amar wouldn't understand, arguing with him is an exercise in futility. Surrender sometimes, has a strength of its own, a strength I draw from and sustain myself with, when I have to.

How I would love to let my hair down and walk down the street in a dirty, faded maxi and shock the entire neighbourhood. What wouldn't I give to wear a halter-neck blouse held together with a string at the nape of my neck with a plain, black silk sari and no jewellery at all. At least, no diamonds. Please, no diamonds. I would love to change my life for that of my tailor's wife down the street. She can wear what she likes to. She has never worn diamonds in her whole life. Nor is she likely to, now or in the future. Her husband does not tailor her clothes. She buys them from the Hawkers Corner at Kalighat. He does not care about what she wears and how. I should know. She lives next door. At 46, rebellion too, is not becoming. Or perhaps, all the jewellery, the saris and the diamonds have slowly, yet surely, sucked away the strength and the will to rebel. I console myself by talking about the 'strength of surrender' which I know, is as foolish as it is fake. Before we are to step into the car outside, I ask for a minute to go to the bathroom. I want this rare moment of private space with myself. He looks at me, falters for a second, and then says, "Fine. But see that you don't take your time about it. We are late already."

When I look at myself in the mirror, I discover that for the first time in all these years, the sparkle in my eyes has extended to cover my entire face. My skin sparkles, so do my lips, my nose, my eyebrows, the *bindi* on the centre of my broad forehead. The diamonds I am wearing with the first initial of my name crafted on each piece, seem to have paled to insignificance next to the brilliance of my face. I allow my unshed tears to flow freely and slowly for the first time in these 25 years. Also, for the last time. Because, I suddenly realise that I have turned into a diamond myself. The diamond with the perfect cut, carat and clarity–without heart, soul, feelings, emotions. My angular face looks like an eightpoint diamond piece, transparent so I can see through the sockets where my eyeballs rest, the bony structure that forms the base of my nose, my cheek bones, my skull, even the china-tiled wall of the bathroom behind me. Yet, I know I am a fake because I have lost, or perhaps never had–the fourth quality that completes the four C's to identify a genuine diamond. The quality I had forgotten about and remember now–Colour. I have no colour left in me anymore. I feel sick inside. I want to throw up in the sink. I cannot, because I am no longer human. Will I make a gift of myself to Reema today to wear as a wedding anniversary present as a pendant on a chain crafted out of platinum? Diamond–the hardest substance on earth that can cut through steel and iron. But then, it has to have the four C's, and I don't have one of them. Will I expect her to carry the baggage of 'aristocracy' forward with me as her constant 'accessory'? Even if I do, I know she will not accept the 'gift' because her father has taught her never to accept a fake, especially when it happens to be a diamond. I am a diamond forever. So what if I am a fake?

# The Handkerchief

"Where's my handkerchief? I cannot find it," cried Reema, as she rummaged impatiently through the drawers of her unkempt wardrobe, her hair all awry, the belt of her nightie hanging loose off her rapidly expanding waistline.

"How should I know where you keep your handkerchieves, for God's sake?" boomed Sandip, in his bass voice, loving the usual impact it had on his wife. This time, though, he was in for a surprise. It did not seem to impress.

Reema straightened herself, leaving the drawers behind her, bras, panties, lace undies hanging sadly out of their rims. She shook her head back to remove those untidy strands of hair that hung all over her forehead, impeding her vision. She looked up imploringly at Sandip, eyes brimming with tears.

"Please help me find it darling. It is very important."

"I'm sorry dear. I just can't. I really have to rush to meet my nine o'clock appointment this morning. We are closing an important deal, you know. I'll buy you a fresh set this evening, there's a dear."

"Why don't you understand, Sandip? I just have to find *this* particular handkerchief. It means something special to me. I just *have* to find it," cried Reema.

By now, the tears spilled over onto her hollow cheeks, smearing the mascara left over from last night, drawing irregular black lines blending into her tears, evolving into the perfect recipe for a marriage-gone-sour. She had forgotten to cream the mascara away. These days, she had been forgetting to cream her face before going to bed. Oh, why in God's name did she wear mascara at all? When, or where did they ever go out to these days? Sandip always came late from work. "Important meeting", "had to stay back for the campaign", "the client did not approve of the presentation so we sat the night through trying to put it right" were the explanations he offered. She did not know why because she never asked. It did not seem to matter. Besides, Reema trusted him completely. She failed to understand what was happening to her. Did all young wives in their first pregnancy feel like this? So down and out? So sick in the guts? So ugly? So utterly hopeless? Why didn't Sandip help her cope with these sudden changes inside and outside her? Why?

Sandip took his wife's outburst with his usual nonchalance. Shrugging his broad shoulders indifferently, he set about turning the bedclothes on the double-sized bed he did not sleep in these days, trying to (pretending to?) look for the evasive square of fabric. 'What a scene she creates for trivialities!' he thought to himself. Handkerchieves. It was all that fellow William Shakespeare's fault! To have raised the *status quo* of this square piece of fabric to create a schism within an already mismatched marriage between a Black Moor of Venice and a delicately fragile White beauty Desdemona that was doomed to failure from the start! If Shakespeare had not written *Othello*, women like Reema who grew up with *Othello* and *Hamlet* would not have attached emotions and nostalgia with a silly piece of cloth that went by the sophisticated terminology of 'handkerchief.' If you lost one, you just took out a fresh one from your stock. Simple. Sooner or later, the 'lost' handkerchief would surface in the most unlikely of places. With Reema, specially, anything was possible. Why, the other day, she had left the peeling knife in the toilet washbasin! Then, one other time, Reema had forgotten her bunch of keys inside the video-case in the living room. And her Rayban glasses inside the fridge!

But Reema seemed to have made a habit of making simple things complicated. How did a handkerchief matter really? There were all kinds of handkerchieves floating around in the market. Coloured and white ones, ones with borders, woven, printed or embroidered. Handkerchieves with scalloped edges, or dainty, lace ones which could only define decoration. Perfumed handkerchieves and handkerchieves smelling of sweat or phlegm, pink, blue, pink-and-blue handkerchieves. Handkerchieves with different days of the week embroidered in one corner. Handkerchieves with lipstick marks and mascara stains. Crumpled handkerchieves or neatly starched, ironed and folded handkerchieves sticking out of the coat pocket of a suited-and-booted executive, like himself! Soft, silk, screen-printed, designer handkerchieves bought off boutiques with matching ties to go with them. Like the packet Reema had gifted him with on their last wedding anniversary.

"So okay. No need to get quite so upset. What colour is it? Is it embroidered and monogrammed with scalloped edges, the kind your sister Runa uses?" he asked, avoiding eye contact. Which was easy because he was now turning the mattress over to look under it.

Reema stood frozen in time and space, at the very spot she was. She defined a visual image of distress, against the backdrop of an open wardrobe, its drawers spilling over with slices of her private person out on display, the tip-tap of the rain outside offering a telling soundtrack of indifference and insularity to the drama within. Even her tears, as if in sympathy, stopped streaking down her unwashed cheeks, the hanging belt of her sloppy nightie the only piece of movement in the room, apart from Sandip's feigned rummaging of the bed. Her eyes bored into his bent back, as she began to take stock of their relationship, questioning it in retrospect. Trying to analyse their marriage of two years. All this took a mere fraction of a second. Wiping those ugly tears away almost unconsciously with the back of her hand, she picked herself up from the dregs she had driven herself into. She patted Sandip's back gently, urging him to rise.

Sandip stiffened. He straightened and turned back to face her. Reema no longer found his towering height overbearing and awesome. Handsome he may be. But what use a husband who did not know what handkerchief his wife used? What *handkerchief*, for God's sake? She rued the hours she had wasted away, laundering, starching and ironing his designer handkerchieves to place them neatly folded in his designer wardrobe, all part of the lavish dowry that came with the designer marriage, purportedly designed out of what *she* thought was love. All this, of course, by courtesy of Reema's affluent parents. She knew the colour, the texture, the make, the age and the size of every single suit, shirt, trousers, shoes, socks, ties and hosiery Sandip used. She knew which pyjama suit of his needed mending or replacement. She knew when his perfume and his after-shave were going to run out and replaced them almost at once, drawing from the handsome savings account her father had opened for her during her marriage to Sandip. She surprised herself with her perfect acumen for evolving into the ideal housewife. Her present disgraceful condition she explained away to her pregnancy. And Sandip did not have the faintest idea of what his wife's handkerchief *looked* like!

"Do you even *know* that your wife is in the habit of *using* handkerchieves, Sandip?" asked Reema. Her voice was soft, so soft, that Sandip could hardly hear her. He stood frozen in his tracks. This was a new Reema he was looking at. Her hair away from her face, her eyes blazing with the freezing cool of ice, her feet planted apart on the floor of the untidy bedroom.

"Of c__c__c__o__u__r__s__s__e I d__d__o, Reema" stammered Sandip, shaken from his complacence for the first time, perhaps, in their two-year marriage. She knew he was lying. He knew that she knew he was lying. Reema's stony face broke into a crooked smile. A smile that looked very close to crying. The smile sent a strange shiver of fear within Sandip. Did she know? *Did* she? How *could* she? "You use monogrammed handkerchieves, like Runa does, don't you?" He asked. The minute the words were out, Sandip knew he had stepped into a trap created by the web of lies he had woven around Reema's love for him, and, more important, the total trust she placed in him. Cobweb, to be precise. What puzzled him was, what was so important about this particular handkerchief? How can handkerchieves be so important in a person's life apart from being a utilitarian square of fabric that sometimes added to the ego of people like himself? Was it a gift from an old flame, he wondered. Is that why it was so important? How did the thought that Reema could have had an affair before they met escape him? Had he taken his dowdy wife too much for granted simply because *he* felt she had become sloppy and loose and dowdy? Was she really the things he thought she was? Did she not have a degree in management accountancy from Harvard with a high-paying job she gave up willingly because he liked a wife who would wait at home for him to come back to?

Suddenly, Sandip began to look at the relationship from a completely new perspective. But, for Reema perhaps, everything seemed to have fallen in place. She had just located the missing pieces of the gigantic jigsaw-puzzle-of-a-marriage she had trapped herself in, wasting two precious years away of her thirty-plus. She decided that this time round, she would not allow her emotions to overshadow her razor-sharp intelligence. Not anymore. She had made the wrong decision when she paid a deaf ear to her father's subtle hints about Sandip as husband material for Reema. No more wrong decisions. So what if she was pregnant. Her sharp brain had already begun to weave a diabolic plan to punish this insensitive, self-centred, lying husband of hers who did not know the meaning of the word 'love'. Or trust, for that matter. For him, it was just any four-letter word. Hate, too, Reema suddenly realised, was a four-letter word. So were 'lust' and 'envy' and 'cool'. She would keep the baby of course. But there were other ways of going about looking for a father. Or bringing it up *without* a father. She deliberately withheld from him the fact that the handkerchief she had misplaced was part of the packet of designer scarves and handkerchieves Sandip had gifted her on her first birthday after their engagement. And he had *forgotten*!

"Its okay," said Reema indifferently, without looking at him, as he stood in the centre of the room like a large-sized cardboard cut-out of himself. "I'll find it myself. You can go back to that meeting of yours. What does a mere handkerchief matter, anyway?" Saying this, she censored any further conversation on the subject by stepping into the attached bathroom. She slammed the door on Sandip's face. She did not notice that one end of the nightie belt stuck stubbornly out of the slammed door. As if it wanted to make peace, refusing to go in and be a part of the slammed-door scenario. The pitter-patter of the rain outside magnified to sudden sounds of cracking thunder and lightning. Sandip did not know whether the sound really came from the rains outside, or whether it came from within himself. Or, whether it was the echo of the slammed door spreading out all over the apartment, rising into a crescendo of fear of the unknown.

# In A Negative Sense

"Did you write up the milk accounts, *bouma*?" Aruna's mother-in-law's voice floated down to her from the kitchen.

"Yes, Maa, I did," Aruna replied from the bedroom, where she was busy tightening a loose button on Somnath's shirt-cuff. Somnath paced the room restlessly in vest and trousers. He was getting late for work.

"Mummy, did you put in some extra sandwiches for Ulka in my tiffin-box?" Aruna's ten-year old daughter came running in to ask, prim and proper in her starched and ironed school uniform. Hair plaited in two tiny little pigtails-in-ribbons she enjoyed swinging this way and that as she moved.

"Yes, my dear, I did. How can I forget your cranky ways, my pet, if I don't do as asked?" Aloka romped away happily, pigtails swinging behind her. Aruna smiled to herself as she tied the final knot, tore off the extra thread with her teeth and handed the shirt to Somnath. He took it from her without a word and began to put it on. They were not on talking terms for the past two days. Somnath often went into these moody bouts of silence without rhyme or reason. In the beginning, it disturbed Aruna. She would go on coaxing and cajoling him to talk. "Say something, please!" "Tell me what I've done to make you so angry." With time, she got used to it. She took it in her stride as one of his endless idiosyncrasies. Of late, it amused her more than annoyed her. How childish it was for two adults to talk in gestures, she thought. For that's what it amounted to. When Somnath stopped talking, it meant that he had just stopped *voicing* his demand. He still mimed out whatever he wished to say, or spoke through Aloka, their daughter. Funnier still, he spoke to the wall. Why didn't he choose to be a mime artist? Aruna wondered at times. He'd have been a winner. Words addressed to the wall, bounced right back at Aruna. Or floated in mid-air, like a wispy cloud. Or, faded away and out of the window of their bèdroom. She took the message, never mind the way it reached her. Aruna had trained herself to carry on wordlessly, till Somnath broke his self-imposed vow of silence himself.

"*Bouma*, will you season the *dal?* I have boiled it already." It was her mother-in-law again, calling her from the kitchen.

"Yes Maa, I am coming," Aruna said. She rose from her bed, covered her head with the end of her sari and went to the kitchen. She placed the *kadai* on the stove, poured oil in it, let it heat up, and then began to temper the *dal*. Three green chillies, slit down the length, a few cummin seeds and cassia leaves, a pinch of asafoetida, alongwith a little sugar. Then a pinch of turmeric. She waited for a few seconds to let them splutter in the smoking oil. Then, she picked up the bowl of boiled *dal* and poured the liquid in. The fresh coriander was chopped and ready. She would add it to the *dal* before she took it off the stove. The sharp aroma of fresh coriander mixed with frying green chillies almost erased the fragrance of Aruna's talcum, generously used after her morning bath. Her mother-in-law's voice came closer. Without looking, Aruna knew she was now inside the kitchen.

"And while you are at it, you might as well chop the vegetables for the curry."

"Yes, *Maa.*"

"And what about little Guddu's bath?" her mother-in-law continued, in the same dictatorial voice. She framed her sentences like questions. But she voiced them like commands. Commands that would not, repeat, *not* brook either defiance or question.

"I'll put the bath water on the boil, Maa," Aruna said. "Guddu is still fast asleep. He has his bath at ten. There is no hurry." Aruna was already at the sink, filling water from the tap into a large-sized *dekchi* to be heated for Guddu's bath.

Aruna's mother-in-law turned back at the kitchen door and looked down at her daughter-in-law. It gave her great pleasure to look down at people. Especially if it happened to be Aruna, her one and only daughter-in-law.

"But you know that the *dhobi* is due at ten with the laundry. Or have you forgotten already?" Her voice had a subtle undertone of menace in it. It was always wasted on goody-goody Aruna.

"I know, Maa," smiled Aruna. "I have kept the clothes, the account book and the money ready."

"And don't forget to cut fruit for your father-in-law's breakfast. He will be going out today." So many 'ands' before she made any statement, thought Aruna to herself. Her mother-in-law wasted both breath and energy by using the conjunction like a prefix. Aruna was sometimes tempted to ask her, "why so many 'ands' Maa?" But then, questioning was something she had never learnt to voice. She *had* questions. But she drank them in. If she wanted answers, she sought these from within herself. "Yours is not to question why, yours is but to do or die" and all that. The quote suited housewives like Aruna better than they suited the fighting soldiers at Kargil.

"Yes, Maa, I will," said Aruna, opening the 'fridge to take out an apple, an orange and a slice of ripe papaya for her father-in-law's breakfast. She took a plate off the shelf, washed, rinsed and dried it with a chequered blue-and-white duster. She washed the fruits too, placed them on the plate, washed a razor-sharp peeler and began to peel the apple.

Sudha, Aruna's college-going sister-in-law, breezed into the kitchen. A little out-of-breath, she asked, "have you kept your green Kancheepuram ironed and laundered, *boudi*? I want to wear it today to the English Lit Social."

"Yes, Sudha. You'll find it on my bed." Sudha scuttled off. It was her emerald green Kancheepuram silk sari with a bright mustard, *zari*-hemmed skirt border. It was one of her richest saris, a part of Aruna's trousseau. But Aruna did not flinch when Sudha borrowed it for special occasions. Never mind that when she came back, Sudha would unfailingly throw the crumpled sari back on Aruna's bed, without caring to fold it back and ready for ironing. "Give them enough rope," her worldly-wise mother repeated when she was getting married, "and they'll let you skip through. Just say 'yes' to everything, everyone, and the rest will follow smoothly, naturally, without dispute or debate," she summed up.

Aruna smiled wistfully at the thought. All of these twelve years, she had given them so much rope that even the world could have skipped through. But not Aruna. No. They kept a tight hold on her all right. Rather, the same rope had ended up tying Aruna into tiny, tight little knots of the small affirmative—*Yes*.

Aruna's mother was no more. From where she now was, she would never guess that, inspite of all her worldly-wise advice, her daughter had not been able to skip through. Aruna had taken her mother's advice so seriously that she had accepted this "yes-woman" role in her life without qualms. She had almost forgotten how the word "no" sounded from her own lips to her own ears. She did hear others say "no" quite often, if not always, mostly, where she herself was concerned. If she asked permission to go for a movie with Somnath, the ma-in-law always said 'no'. When she once asked Somnath for a holiday in the hills, he said 'no'. When she asked the servant-boy to fetch something-in-a-hurry, he did not say 'no' but he did an equally negative thing. He pretended not to have heard. A clever way of defying orders without getting caught. As far as Aruna was concerned, she said "yes" to everything, to everyone, all the time. The word, for her, was now more a reflex action than a word with meaning. Her conversations began, ended or were centred round the one affirmative monosyllable. YES. Never mind whether she was addressing the servant or was talking to her father-in-law in revered tones.

Aruna often recalled having read about the *Sabar* tribes in the Bengal-Bihar border in India. They only whisper because they do not like to reveal their presence. They wish to keep away from the police and from the so-called civilised society. They never say 'yes' ever. But they say 'no' very easily. Instead of saying 'yes,' they make some kind of frightening sound. Anthropologists say there was a time when these suppressed people could not say 'no' because they were not allowed to. Not even when they were opposed to something with their heart and soul. For them therefore, 'yes' was a meaningless word. Maybe, that is how 'yes' has become a negative sound instead of a positive word. But Aruna was determined to sustain the positive implications of 'yes'. Diametrically opposed to the *Sabars*, she had neatly clipped the 'no' out of her everyday vocabulary.

Aruna knew that the younger wives in the neighbourhood contemptuously called her "Mrs. Yes" behind her back. Aruna did not mind. She was used to playing second fiddle so much that the desire to hog the limelight just did not occur to her. She was content to take a backseat and let others take centrestage. She preferred submission to assertion. Didn't it do away with the myriad complications life-as-it-is was beset with? Didn't it rob her mother-in-law and her self-righteous husband of the excuse of pointing that invisible accusing forefinger at her for the flimsiest of non-reasons? It certainly made for comparatively peaceful surroundings at home. There were enough of warring "no's" resounding around her all the time. At least there was one person who kept away from this eternal, internal warfare. She never quarrelled with Somnath, never. She did not argue with anyone, not even with the quick-tempered Sudha, who was much younger than Aruna. She never answered her mother-in-law back. Aruna knew that in this very submission, lay her final triumph. Her subdued "yes" role made her almost totally indispensable to the family. It was always "*Bouma* this" or "*boudi* that" or "Aruna, where are you?"

If one wished to conjure up a mental picture of Aruna, it wouldn't be difficult. One would just have to close one's eyes to visualise a pretty young wife in her mid-thirties, sari worn Bengali style with the end draped twice over the left shoulder, the inevitable bunch of keys jingling away happily, head slightly covered with the end of the sari, the dot of vermilion on her forehead smudged in sweat, a few strands of hair running wild, away from the face. She scuttled in soft-footed, hurried steps from the kitchen to the dining room to the living room to the bathroom—fetching and carrying, tending and caring, obeying and serving with an ever-smiling face—conversation mostly confined to the happy three letter word "Yes."

Aruna was the ideal of all the mothers-in-law in the neighbourhood. She was a Utopian reality. She was a dream-come-true and she knew it. Women in the neighbourhood were jealous of her mother-in-law. They felt she was too lucky to have got a subservient and an ever-acquiescent daughter-in-law who was a fairy-tale-come-true. Somnath's friends envied him too. None of them had a wife who performed her duties silently, never nagged her husband for this *sari* or that film, and never questioned him about late nights to make him feel guilty. Somnath gloated about his obedient wife quite brazenly to his office colleagues. He said he had a wife who expected nothing, but nothing in return. Aloka adored her mother. *Her* mother was not like her friends' mothers whose conversations with their children were amply sprinkled with "no's" and "don'ts." *Her* mother always said "Yes". Aloka knew she was spoilt rotten—that's what her friends were telling her all the time. She was happy all the same. Did it not give her that feeling of being one-up on all her friends, who, she knew, were that wee bit jealous?

Aruna was rubbing turmeric and salt into the chopped vegetables to cook the vegetable stew for Guddu and his grandpa when she heard a knock on the front door. Something was wrong with the doorbell and Somnath had not done one thing about it. Her father-in-law was having his bath. Somnath, she guessed, was dolling himself up in front of the mirror. Bhola, the servant, was taking his own sweet time in the market, gossiping away to his heart's content. Her mother-in-law was folding her day's quota of *paans*. She never answered the door when Aruna was there to answer it. Aruna quickly wiped her turmeric-stained fingers on her sari-front and went to open the door.

The postman held out a sheaf of letters. Two bills for her father-in-law. A letter from the insurance company for Somnath. One letter for her mother-in-law from Delhi, where her elder daughter lived. An invitation card addressed to Sudha. The last one was addressed to Aruna. It was a longish envelope with foreign stamps. With a transparent 'window' in front through which she could read her full name and address. Aruna was surprised. No one ever wrote to her. Her parents were no more. Her only brother Amit, who lived in Detroit with his American wife, sent her short notes jotted on the back of picture-postcards at Bijoya Dasami, Naba Barsha, Christmas, New Year, Aruna's birthday. Aruna did not mind the cursory dryness of the communication. She and Amit were emotionally too close to bother about keeping track of each other through formal letters. Aruna looked at the letter closely through the 'window'. Her name and address were a computer printout. She gingerly tore open one end of the envelope with nervous fingers. There must be some mistake, she thought. She hoped it wasn't bad news.

There was no mistake. Nor was it 'bad news'. The letter, without mincing words, offered her a visiting lectureship next Fall in "Indian Writing in English by Indo-Anglian Women Writers" at the Cornell University in the US for three months. Aruna stood rooted to the spot. Slowly, realisation began to dawn. She had forgotten she had a Ph.D. in English Literature. She had forgotten about all the Indo-Anglian writers she had once specialised in—Nayantara Sahgal, Anita Desai, Kamala Markandaya, Zohra Futehally, and the rest of the lot. In fact, she had almost forgotten their names! She had also forgotten that, about a year back, during one of Somnath's longest phases of silence lasting a fortnight, out of frustration in a marriage trapped within a prison of one single word, she had wanted to break out of the vicious circle of "Yes". Never mind that she had done it herself. In an impulsive, spontaneous act of rebellion, she had applied in answer to a newspaper ad for a lectureship. And forgotten about it the minute Somnath signed truce. Amit, dear Amit, her darling brother, hadn't forgotten. He had safely guarded her documents and testimonials all these years. Aruna had sent a copy of her application to Amit with a covering letter informing him of her application. In the rigmarole of her daily chores of wilful submission to feudal demands, within those intense moments of passion with Somnath, those deep moments of affection for Aloka, all sandwiched and framed neatly within a cobweby trap of "yes's," the single act of secret defiance had quietly slipped her memory.

Amit also seemed to remember Aruna's secret dream of working for a short stint at a foreign university just for the "feel" of it. Feel. That's a nice word, thought Aruna to herself. But Aruna had forgotten what 'feel' was all about. Memories of a happy and young past, memories of sparring with a kid brother, flooded her mind in a rush. It was filled with 'feelings'. Many kinds of feelings. Good and bad feelings. Happy feelings and sad feelings. Feelings with colour and music and smell. Feelings you could almost touch, as you touched that teddy dad bought you on your fifth birthday, or your first water bottle you took along at kindergarten. For Aruna, all 'feelings' were reduced to the lowest common denominator of 'yes'. She used 'yes' like an insulation against feelings of all kinds. 'Yes' to her, was a defence mechanism, an instrument of compliance, a utilitarian tool and an escape route, all at the same time. For her, 'feelings' were sacrificed to the logistics and the mechanics of one monosyllable, 'yes'. Her brother Amit though, still seemed to have kept hold on feelings. Feelings that were coloured and were fragrant and could be heard, read, understood, felt. He easily felt from across the seven seas, his sister's willful sacrifice of her academic brilliance to cobwebs of time, space, and duty. Unknown to herself, Aruna had surrendered to the weighty role of the Ideal-Indian-Daughter-in-law of an Ideal-Indian-Hindu-Joint-Family. The surprising letter and the application must have thrilled Amit. He took upon himself, the onerous task of rescuing her, at least for some time, from the vacant abyss of domestic drudgery that had reduced her to anonymity. He followed up the application with tunnel vision—till he saw she got the job. So what if it was one year too late? Time did not matter to women like Aruna. Space did. He knew and he understood. And he *felt* for Aruna like no one in *this* family did. The letter mentioned Dr. Amitabh Bhattacharjee's reference and recommendation.

She read the typed, crisply worded lines over and over again till she felt the sharp sting of tears in her eyes. Were they tears of happiness? Or, were they tears of sorrow? Perhaps, they were tears of relief? At that moment, she could not decide which. She was in a hurry to hide her tears before they threatened to streak down her perspiring cheeks. Aruna did not have the typical Indian-womanly habit of crying in public, even in front of the immediate family. She quickly wiped her moist eyes with the end of her sari. She read and re-read the letter till she had memorised it. Suddenly, she heard Somnath clear his throat, right behind her. It was *his* way of telling her that the 'silent' phase was over. She turned around with a smile. Her eyes swept him from head to feet. He had his tie in place. The starched whiteness of his shirt certified Aruna's perfection as a wife. His face was powdered. And he smelt strongly of the aftershave she was so used to. Finally, her eyes came to rest on his face. She held the letter out under his nose, pointing her index finger to the 'to' address. Somnath did not even look at it. His eyes were fixed on Aruna's face. Looking deep into those just-wet, sparkling eyes, he said, "I've read it already over your shoulder. But what's the great point?" Shrugging indifferently before he turned to the door, he said,

"Throw away the letter. Or keep it if you wish to. It does not matter. Because you aren't accepting the appointment."

As always, it was a statement, not a question. Coming from Somnath, it mattered little, whether it was a statement, or a question. It meant the same thing. Command, and its unquestioned acceptance. For once, for all the strength the statement appeared to exude, Aruna suddenly wondered — wasn't the 'confidence' in Somnath's voice laced with a subtle note of fear? And uncertainty, perhaps? For once, Aruna answered the statement with a question. She walked around to face him, looked right back into his eyes and asked, "Why not?" Then, just to keep the record straight, without preamble, she said, "Yes, Somnath, I *am* accepting it."

For the first time in her married life, Aruna was surprised to find what happiness, and strength, and courage, that single word could give her. All feelings she thought had vanished into eternity, came flooding right back. 'Yes' was no longer a meaningless word used to sustain peace and order. It was a word full of colour and smell and touch and remembrance of happy times. It was a live word full of sound and fury that could reveal any human emotion depending on how it was used, when, where, most importantly – by whom. It was a fluid word, a liquid soundbyte that could turn the pivot of one's life full circle, or take it completely in the opposite direction. It was as unpredictable as an angry river in full spate that takes people and their loves alongwith it, destroying them forever, purging itself of God-knows-what-or-why. It was like the softhallowed, silvery shimmer of moonlight that gently caresses the one who uses it and the one it is used on. It was like the Rubik's Cube, that could be turned to fit in two minutes flat, or could never be matched at all. It could be used in a negative sense. Just like 'no' was often used in a positive sense. With a single stroke, without disturbing the *status quo* of her vocabulary, Aruna had dramatically toppled the *status quo* of her life. Aruna was surprised to discover how, without even being aware of it, she had turned the word *yes* into a weapon of rebellion.

# Love (Letters) On A Mellow Afternoon

*My Darling Runu,*

*Which way will the tide turn when you arrive this Sunday to my city? Do you think of me all the time like I do? Do you ever see me, talk to me, touch me, kiss me in your dreams? Does that shivering dewdrop on the rhododendron leaf remind you of how you shivered when I touched you that first time in the dimly lit staircase of the college on our Annual Day with no one watching us? Do you look out of the window of your room, right next to your desk, to gaze at nothing in particular because your thoughts are full of me, me and me? Do you still keep that clandestinely clicked picture of you and me hidden in the pages of your favourite Shakespeare? Does the hooting engine of an approaching long-distance train make you desperately wish I was in one of the bogies, coming to see you, touch you, feel you, kiss you? Do you always think of me whenever you wear blue, my favourite colour? Are there a few drops left of that imitation perfume I gave you for your birthday because I could not afford anything more expensive? How do you explain not having written to me for eight weeks now? How do you explain that even then, we can still communicate telepathically with each other? How do you explain that gut feeling I had of your having tripped on your saree and hurt yourself so bad that you were immobile for two weeks? Do you know how my heart bleeds over the distance that is keeping us apart? Do you too, feel the same way? Do you understand that my entire existence is now focussed on just one single thought—to take you away to the hills forever, away from all prying eyes save my own? Do you understand how crazy I feel when I fail to pluck clouds off that azure blue sky to lay them at your feet? Do you? Do you Runu? Do you?*

*Yours, forever and ever,*
*Dilip.*

Ronita folded the letter with great care, so that the wearied folds did not give way and reduce it into fragmented bits of decimated nostalgia. The paper, once white, was now yellowed over twenty years of opening, reading, re-reading, musing over, day-dreaming, folding back, over and over again. The ink, too, had faded. Unevenly. She could still read through each letter because she had got the words by heart. She wore a wistful smile. The lower cups of her eyes were moist with unshed tears.

Another letter strung words like tiny little flowers, to weave a beautiful garland of love.

My Darling Heart-throb,

*A pressed rose tucked into the pages of a Wordsworth. A Tagore love song floating in from the neighbouring house. Munching roasted peanuts tossed in salt and chilli powder while waiting for you to make your usual timid, shy, belated appearance. Sensing your arrival from the fragrance of the inexpensive perfume I gave you. Crying like a spoilt baby after a squabble over who is going to pay the bill at the Irani restaurant. Feeling the breeze kiss our faces as we share silence on the beach at Shivaji Park on a Sunday evening. Penning love-notes in the office when the boss is not looking. Throwing over-the-shoulder looks to see if someone is watching as I hook my confident-shy elbow into your soft, tender one. Walking hand-in-hand, barefeet, into the beach waters and feeling the surf kiss our ankles. Searching that single lost ear-ring we dropped together on the sands and not being able to find it. Chanting a Shakespeare sonnet together on a rainy day. Fighting over an omelette in the smelly cabin of a small restaurant. Counting coins at the end of the day to see if there is money left for the bus-ride back home. Reading your letters over and over again when you are away on that hated interview. Sucking the blood off my fingers while getting cut at the kitchen table, chopping onions, because my mind was elsewhere, traversing the streets of Delhi, with you. Alas! How long will I have to go on dreaming up these scenes that never happened, my Desdemona? I have neither given nor taken any handkerchief from you monogrammed with my name on it, delicately embroidered with silken strands in blue and with the passion of your fragile-soft hands, my darling Dessy. Then why do you hurt me so with your silence? I promise you there never was, nor is, and neither will be any Iago to ruin the dream-castle of our happiness. I have faith in you darling Desdemona. Complete and total faith. Shakespeare is dead. Long live Shakespeare.*

*Yours, perchance to dream?*
*Othello*

The skin of her work-rough hands stood out in goose pimples. This letter, and those others in the pink-ribboned packet she kept hidden in her wardrobe, smothered with mothballs, evolved into a single note of hope in her tuneless, colourless life. Ronita placed the letter back in the packet and picked out another. She felt that slight tremor in her hands she had become used to, each time she picked one of the dozen-and-odd letters to read, re-read, memorise, reflect on, if only to feel sorry for herself. And hopeful, at the same time.

*My Anarkali,* began another letter, the last one in the pack. It was place-marked Dilli, dated back to the time of the Moghul rule during the reign of Akbar-the-Great.

*I vow to break asunder any brick wall that comes between the two of us and our intense love for each other. I promise to caress your beautiful face with the petals of the biggest and the most fragrant rose from my father's royal garden. The same father who hates to see us united forever and in love. I assure you that no harem will ever threaten your sole monopoly over my feelings for you. I will never recognise any Noor Jehan except through the pages of Moghul history. Did*

*I tell you I saw **Anarkali** (the film) twelve times and **Mughal-e-Azam** (the film) for twice that number? All this, after I set eyes on you? On video? I'll let you in on a secret. Once, I took myself to Maganlal Dresswalla's at Kalbadevi to hire a costume that would fit the historical character of Salim, just to find out how irrational my fantasising was. When they asked me if I wanted it for theatre, I told them the truth. "I want to see whether I suit the Anarkali of my life. I want my life to be a real-life dream." They looked at each other and laughed. I would have also hired the Anarkali dress for you. We would have got ourselves photographed for memory at the local studio. But you were in Delhi being 'looked at' which I did not then know. When I came home with the parcel under my arm, my mother calmly placed your wedding card in my unsuspecting palm. I threw the parcel away in the pond at the back of our house. I never went back to Maganlal Dresswalla's again. When they asked for the money, I sent it by post. Where are you, my Anarkali? Why did they trap you and bury you within the four walls of a suffocating marriage you never wanted in the first place? Did I vow to break all walls asunder? I can't anymore. Because marriage creates walls that are not bricklined. These are invisible walls solidly bound by values a modern-day Salim cannot dare break unless his Anarkali steps out on her own. I **know** you will not, even if you can.*

*Never ever again yours,*
*Salim*

Each letter wove one romantic fantasy after another, endlessly, eternally, creating an emotionally rich, designed, luminous carpet out of the textured imagination of Dilip's rosy dreams. Dilip took on the persona of Arjuna and wrote to Draupadi about his feelings of anger and pain, and regret, when she went those other nights to be made love to, by his four Pandava brothers, leaving him alone to pine for her, in helpless rage and unfulfilled passion. In another letter, he became the Lord Krishna, penning a letter to Radha with the pointed end of his magic flute, signing it with his thumbprint dyed in blood. Devdas wrote to Parvati, with his pen dipped in pseudo-alcohol, quoting from a Saigal song from the New Theatres' film. There was one letter from Robert Browning to his lady-love, Elizabeth, place-marked 'Wimpole Street'. And one from William Shakespeare to Anne Hathaway at Stratford. Ronita created enough time, and space, to read them at least once, every single day. For that hour-and-odd, she felt herself mesmerised into the hypnotic trance of romantic fantasy. Or, was it fantasised romance? It really did not matter which, except that the letters wove a magic veil around her, like Cinderella's pumpkin-turned-chariot-turned-pumpkin, even if it was to bring her to the earthiness of reality bumping back again.

As she tied the pink ribbon for the last time that evening, Ronita felt that gentle, familiar tap on her shoulder. "How many times will you read the same letters, Rooni?" asked her husband, Aniket, with that smug smile of amused tolerance he used so casually on her. She smiled back, but did not answer. "How about the mandatory cup of tea, Rooni?" She placed the packet back in the wardrobe, locked it and tucked the bunch of keys in the belt of her shapeless, faded, maxi. With a sigh she did not care to hide, she moved towards the kitchen. As she put the kettle on the boil and took the tea-tin off the shelf, she felt sorry for Aniket. She added sugar to the cups, put in a dash of milk and waited for the water to boil over. She thought of her life with her 'propah', foreign-returned, corporate CEO husband.

Twenty years. Twenty years of life together, sans children, sans honeymoon, (he had an important seminar soon after, so no time) sans holidays, ("no time") sans romance, ("we aren't teenagers, so stop being foolish and acting like one") sans conversation, (newspapers, BBC-news-on-the-telly, papers-brought-back-from-work-to-be-pored-over-at-night.) He never wrote letters when he went on tours abroad ("you know I am a computer-person and hate to put pen on paper to compose emotional nonsense.") He sent faxes or made inane telephonic conversations that were as clipped and as dry as the paper flowers in their drawing room vase.

Trring trring trring.

"Hello. Who's there?"

"Its me, Aniket. Is that Ronita? How are you?"

"Fine, how about you? How was the flight?"

"I'm okay. The flight was swell. Bought you a bottle of *Channel No. 5*. Or would you have preferred *Poison*? Don't forget to pay the newspaperman the bill, will you?"

"Hmmm. When are you getting back?"

Pause. Pause.

"Can't say right now. Got to rush off to a meeting. Ring you back at night from the hotel. Bye."

Pause. Pause.

"Why don't you answer?"

Silence.

"Bye."

"Bye."

Click.

Silence.

The slight flutter of pigeons who had decided to perch themselves on Ronita's window-sill made a sunny hole into the dark silence after the telephone clicked off.

He might as well have had the lines taped and inserted into a mobile answering machine. He brought her the mandatory foreign perfumes. He did not forget to point out, though, that he had bought them off the in-flight duty-free trays on board his flights. So there was no particular brand she could make a habit of. They never ate junk food off roadside stalls. ("It is bad for our health, remember?") She could not remember having shared ice-cream cones with Aniket on city streets, with dollops of cream pouring down their laughing chins. ("It's bad for the tonsils.") Dinners and lunches out were always at pricey, ornamental hotels where the waiters moved silently like robots without a hint of human expression on their poker faces. Where the menu cards were so clean and so large that you had to turn the pages gingerly so you did not dirty them. Where the hot crockery and the clutter of cutlery were enough to scare you off your appetite. Where the names of dishes were borrowed from plush restaurants in Spain and Italy and France and you did not understand what they meant since you did not know those languages. So you ordered from gut feeling or if the name sounded promising. And the dish took you completely by unpleasant surprise. Where the lighting was so dim that you never knew what you were really eating and could be eating octopus when you had ordered chicken. Where Ronita was forced to watch hungrily as other couples cavorted gracefully on the dance floor because Aniket did not quite care for dancing. Decency prevented her from dancing with strangers. Decency, *not* desire. After dinner got over and the dance continued, they sat and watched. Ronita closed her palms into tight little fists and held them under the table, on her lap, to stop herself from clapping to the beat of the music. Wives with husbands like Aniket learnt fast to gain the strength and the skill *not* to articulate their intimate desires. In bed. Or out of it.

Movies? Yes, they took them in once in a while, at screenings at the corporate club of which Aniket was a revered member. But they were arty-arty French films and Italian films and British films that had won awards at Cannes or San Sebastian or Berlin. They always made Ronita struggle against dozing off because she found them very, v-e-r-y b—o—r—i—n—g. She was brought up on a generous diet of Hindi *masala* films. She loved the song-and-dance routine, the dream sequences shot in tulip gardens in Holland or at the dolphin parks in Australia or on the snowcapped mountains in Switzerland. She felt more comfortable with Amitabh Bachchan's anger in *Deewar* or Dilip Kumar's naughtiness in *Naya Daur* than with the architectural design in an Antonioni film or the electric intensity of a Wim Wenders' masterpiece. She did suggest *Sholay* once. But Aniket gave her a look that made his reaction transparent enough for her to give up her suggestive habit for good. Ronita loved make-believe. She adored fairy tales and as a child, enjoyed weaving imaginary castles out of thin air and vivid, colourful imagination. What was wrong with make-believe? Everything, according to

Aniket. He said it all with that slight inflection in his golden-honey, cultivated voice, briefly, editing away needless vocabulary, complemented by the piercing look in his black, bright pupils centrally placed in those almond-shaped eyes.

He was not familiar with Tagore at all because he had studied at Nainital and could neither read nor write Bengali. ("I don't need to learn Bengali because I am never going to use it.") Nor did he involve himself in the famous dramatic events there, because he had decided to make science and engineering his forte. ("Naseeruddin Shah was in my class. He chose well because he did become an actor, didn't he?") He listened to music of course. But it had to be Chopin or Mozart or Beethoven or some similar Western Classical symphony. He made concessions to a Bade Ghulam Ali Khan or a Pandit Ravi Shankar or Girija Devi once in a while. But Ronita did not find them entertaining at all. She revelled in the old Hindi numbers of *eena-meena-deeka* and *man dole* and *tu pyar ka sagar hai*.

He smiled and laughed a lot, though. Sometimes with Ronita, mostly *at* her. Many a time, at her foolish fascination for literature—English, Bengali, Hindi. At her craze for Hindi films and film songs. Made jokes too. This made life somewhat *bearable*. Life with Aniket taught Ronita that a sugary, 'propah' husband could also, *unwittingly*, indulge in clinically designed but totally unintended, emotional torture through the simple strategy of slighting her, sidetracking her, marginalising her—oh so subtly! By sustaining a stiff, British upper lip, even if his studies had been conducted totally in India before he had ever set eyes on Queen's country. He could make his wife sick —like the sickness one feels in the gut after an over-generous helping of cloyingly sweet rose syrup labelled Rooh Afza or anything else, or Cadbury's chocolates. A torture from which there is no escape, because there is no law against it. A torture that cannot be corrected by counselling either, because it is invisible, shapeless, abstract, ambivalent, irreversible. To outward appearances, you are the ideal couple. But there is always, an alternative, subtly cruel, politically understated reality lurking behind the seeming-Utopia. An Utopia from which Ronita had discovered a temporary escape. She found them in the packet of letters.

Aniket did not know those letters were not hers at all. She allowed him to go on believing what he wished to. With that, she hoped to arouse in him, at least *some* feelings of envy, of possessiveness, which could perhaps, infuse their marriage with the magic of romance that was JustNotThere. Could make him share with her, even now, that ice-cream cone to allow the cream to drip down their ageing chins. To eat *pani puri* and *pav-bhaji* off a roadside stall only to fall sick together, just in case. To watch *Hum Dil De Chuke Sanam* snuggling close, with her head on his shoulder, on the back row of a full, darkened theatre. To listen to a loud jazzy number being belted out on MTV, a channel Aniket hated and Ronita loved.

The letters were penned by Dilip, her older sister Rohini's lover. He committed suicide a year after Rohini (Runu) got married to someone else. The secret offered Ronita the romantic palliative she so desperately missed. She enjoyed the puncture to Aniket's ego. The thought that he was neither the first, nor the only man in his wife's life must hurt him. It must shake his super-complacent super-ego in some small way, which, she knew, he hid behind that smug smile of pseudo-confidence. In some strange way, Ronita, 45, had fallen in love with the Dilip-of-the-letters, a Dilip she had never met nor known, except through these yellowed letters that brought love to her in the mellow afternoon of her life. Would the letters help infuse new life into their own twenty-year-old, near-dead marriage? Perhaps they would. Perhaps they wouldn't. At this point of time, it did not matter. Really.

# My Kitchen, My Space

*The motion of the wasted world accelerates just before the final precipice.*
—William Faulkner, from *As I Lay Dying*

"The kitchen is too small!" she says, to no one in particular. She throws the words in the air like a ball. Is it a statement? It is definitely not a question. Youngsters these days rarely ask questions. Why should they? When they think they know all the answers? They are ever eager to attack you with answers even when no questions have been asked. To my trained ears therefore, the statement sounds more like an accusation. Like a habit that has grown on women like me. I catch the accusation in mid-air like a skilled fielder. I tuck it into my blouse, as if it is something I need to hide. As if, having a small kitchen is my fault. Perhaps, also of their leaving this place to move out someplace else. As if, the size of the kitchen is squarely responsible for splitting a complete family horizontally into two equal halves, one young, one old, reflecting the transgenerational gap between parents and their grownup children. I respond, in my way, with silence. Quiet submission has a habit of growing on you. Thirty years of it is more than half a life, when one is fifty years old.

Submission does not imply surrender, though it could mean that you are keeping your thoughts to yourself while pretending to submit to other people's thoughts and wishes. It gives the one who makes you submit a feeling of one-upmanship, complacence, and false patrony. Submission, for me, is keeping my responses to myself, and then going ahead and airing it somewhere else. Where I have created a space of my own. My space is my kitchen. My kitchen has been my space for 25 years. It will remain my little island of private sunshine as long as I remain alive.

"The kitchen is too small," said my husband, when we first stepped into this flat. He sounded a bit apologetic about it. "You'll find it a bit stuffy to work in," he went on. I looked around the tiny, raised platform, the sink in the corner, the shelves on the top, then squeezed my heavy frame in to find out: "Yes. It is a bit small," I said to myself. To him, I said, "It's all right. I'll manage." I managed all right. Management of my kitchen space became the central focus of my life. I hardly realised how critical a role it played in my evolution as woman, mother, wife, *et al*. Much less did the others in my family. I managed so beautifully, that, in course of time, I became the manager, sole-proprietor, accountant, clerk and watchman of this space, guarding it fiercely like the furry, angry, howling mother-cat fiercely guarding her litter under the staircase of our block of flats. Over time, I forgot that long ago, the two of us had agreed that the kitchen was too small. The kitchen was a part of the world that belonged only to me. I permitted others to step in, but movements in and out were strictly within my control.

I love the smells that kiss and caress and hug me when I enter this small world I own. I have squeezed in a tiny altar on one side of the narrow wall, raised enough for me to be able to place my tiny little gods and goddesses. I offer them little joss sticks and garlands strung out of tiny flowers. A strange mixture of raw, powdered spices blends into the fragrance of lighted joss sticks, mingling with smoking mustard oil on the stove as I season the *masoor ki dal*. Minced onions, two green chillies sliced down their length, two mashed pods of garlic, a tomato diced into tiny bits. Toss them into the steaming oil and wait for the sizzle. The smell turns sharp and pungent. But it also blends into the odour of the gas from the cylinder under the platform, trying to spoil the fun. Like the villain in a Hindi *masala* film. I erase it out when I pour the boiled *dal* in, sprinkle freshly chopped coriander and the fragrance is heady, strongly appetising. I am used to all this.

At times, I keep the window open to let the breeze in. The breeze is the only outsider I welcome into my private domain. If it is a bit too strong, it disturbs the blue flame on the gas stove that flickers, trembles like a shy bride on a nuptial night, and goes out. I have to then shut the window all over again. The cloyingly sweet smell of the washing detergent for cleaning vessels leaves behind its own trace when the maid leaves after her chores. Add to this the stink of the drain, holding remnants of yesterday's cooking—unwashed, forgotten.

The fragrances and odours of nostalgia are forever. I remember throwing up in this sink, again and again, hating the sour smell and loving it at the same time because the smell told me that I was pregnant again. As I empty a leftover bowl of curds into the sink to wash it away, I recall that first day of the smell of inner wastes coming out. I was going to become a mother, all over again. We moved into this flat when Sumit was five. Ten months after we moved in here, I was expecting Smita.

I open the gleaming, stainless steel box of ground turmeric. The smell reminds me of my trial-and-error lessons in cooking, honed over the years by the eager palates of an ever-hungry family. The sharp smell of turmeric brings back memories of another day. The day I discovered I could hurl abuses into this box just by opening the lid, pouring my entire vocabulary of invective into it and then closing the lid tight. The invective was directed towards whomever I was angry at, at that time. It did nothing to expand my vocabulary. But it did help me evolve a kind of tangible, person-to-person relationship with that small, gleaming tin. It knows my secrets. It never leaks them. Not even through my cooking.

I hid a secret lover in the bottle of Horlicks I used to stock my cassia leaves in. *Tej patti*, they call it in the local lingo. It is a very important ingredient for seasoning or soaking in dishes both sweet and savoury. This bottle got more than its regular quota of heart pouring. The leaves have a slightly heady fragrance, just the right kind to hide a secret lover to hold secret conversations with. This, when no one was at home and I was feeling depressed and did not know why. The lover changed from time to time. It was the Nawab of Pataudi in the beginning. He took me out of my depression within seconds when he whispered into my ears the wrong choice of life-mate he had made by choosing Sharmila Tagore, that famous film star, over me. Had he met me before he met her, he would surely have married me. I did not have the heart to set him right. I did not tell him that I was already married when he was courting her. Day-dreaming inside an open bottle of dried, shrivelled up cassia leaves with its slightly heady fragrance has an air of romance about it that calendar errors made by a secret lover do not have. Thoughts of a clandestine affair between two adults, each one married to someone else, holds the potential for adventure and thrill for everyone. I was no different. I found it more thrilling because I was experiencing it myself! Never mind about the vicarious nature of the experience through the agency of cassia leaves. Being part of a daytime fantasy, it fit perfectly into my own notions of middle-class marital morality.

I changed my lovers quite often, quite shamelessly, unknown to the one I was married to. Not once did I suffer pangs of guilt, real or imaginary. But, one wearies of lovers too, never mind how much they sizzle with sex or glimmer with glamour. When I was 45, I began to drop them, one by one —Michael Caine, Rajesh Khanna, Robin Cook, Michael Douglas, Alain Delon, Vinod Mehra, Ted Hughes and Amitabh Bachchan. They were as transient and as fragile as soap bubbles. They floated in the air, then slowly withered away, or burst into nothing.

My tears I hid in the large salt jar. That was easy because salt absorbs moisture. The choice was not by design though. Yet, I did realize that housewives have this deviously innovative psyche that easily tends to link culinary spices and condiments to their own thoughts in everyday life and experience. With time, I found an easier, more public outlet for my tears. I discovered that chopping lots and lots of onions served the same purpose. This blended the real tears with the biological ones, springing forth from the sharp pungency of chopped onions. Strong, sharp and pungent seasonings of dry red and hot chillies in smoking oil served the same purpose. But this could also bring along bouts of sneezing. Chillies are culturally linked to anger and revenge. I managed to make the smooth connection with tears, pain and disillusionment.

The kitchen sink is another exit point for crying and weeping. When you turn the tap open, the water begins to run, making it easier to have your tears mingle with the running water. It also helps drown the sound of crying and hiccuping at the same time. This is precisely why I have taken upon myself, the monotonous chore of washing the sink. I do not feel it is monotonous. I have discovered, to my pleasant surprise, that the vigorous scrubbing of the corners, the strained attempt to wipe out those obstinate black stains, has a miraculous, therapeutic effect on an overstressed nervous system. If there is a big quarrel when people have been slowly and steadily chopping bits and pieces off me, without either trying or wanting to, I rush into my kitchen. I pick up the sponge to attack the sink with it. Even when it is as clean and as washed as a dead body readied for post-mortem. This absolves me of the need to purge my energy on arguments, questions, discussion and debate. I listen, I cry, I abuse, I laugh and I scream. But I do it in my own little world, the kitchen. And no one knows.

Anger. How often, for how many reasons, real and imaginary, do I get angry? The maid does not turn up. Sumit did not score well in the final exams. My husband forgot, by incident or design, to hand me the pay packet on pay-day. These, and many more tiny things could trigger anger. I am angry even with myself if I get a dish wrong and must flush it down the toilet to start all over again. Simple, complex reasons. Straightforward, devious reasons. I am furious with myself for getting into this permanent mode of submission, surrender, even abandon, perhaps, by my own volition. Because I shy away from confrontation. I have evolved into a docile creature, part woman, part animal, bending over backwards not to ruffle feathers that ruffled easily, or with time.

Do all women vent their anger in the kitchen? I have heard stories focussed on women letting off steam with diabolic intent in their kitchens. Some housewives, I have heard, add more salt than needed to what they cook. Some buy off a whole kilo of bitter gourd and cook it without taking the bitterness out. I go one better. I use sound as an expression of anger. I have termed it 'my own noise pollution in the kitchen'. I bang a pair of kitchen pliers just to make the sound echo around the apartment. Never mind that I have to pick it up myself. I use the ladle to stir the curry, making a lot of noise while doing it. Sound, I have learnt with time, can irritate, jar, shock, sometimes even infuse fear. I keep stir-frying, sautéing, boiling, currying my anger, my despair, my disillusionment with the institution of marriage alongwith the French fries, the parboiled vegetables, the jacket potatoes, the fish-curry-in-hot-mustard paste, the pepper-chilli chutneys.

Somewhere along the way, I have stir-fried myself a bit, sliced off a part of my inner self to stack it on the kitchen shelf alongwith my spices, my utensils, my cleaning powders. I have sautéed myself with the growth of my children, till I realized it was all for nothing. I have parboiled myself, bit by painful bit, with those capsicums, carrots, spring onions and celery tossed with a little soya sauce and chilli vinegar for the steaming hot mixed noodle soup till I began to smell a lot like the kitchen myself. I carry bits and pieces of the kitchen on myself, on my clothes, stained with turmeric, chilli powder and drops of cooking oil. I smell a lot of milk, some chilli-tomato curry and fish put together. The dot in the centre of my forehead is a-blur with gleaming beads of perspiration on my face. Strands of curly hair fall across my forehead, sticking to the beads of sweat that I wipe away with the back of my hand, covered with dollops of half-kneaded flour.

Many a night, when the house went to sleep, I kept awake finishing off the last pages of Sidney Sheldon's mushy thriller *Bloodline*. I brought my reading onto my kitchen platform, pulling in one of the dining stools for a seat. I have completed some of my daughter's chemistry journals on the eve of her high school finals on this platform. If the heat caught on, I opened the shutters of the tiny window, it's net eaten into by an interloping, nonchalant rat, allowing the breeze to come in. I have gone on a wild identity-hunting spree with Robert Ludlum's hero in *Bourne Identity*, across the world, coming to rest at the sound of the discordant, disturbing sound of the doorbell ringing in the morning milk. I have gone on long trips to Europe, met the Queen at Buckingham Palace, watched the changing of the guards and revelled in my imagination as the milk cooker merrily kept on ringing warnings of boiling over the stove.

The knives, choppers, slicers, graters, cooking ladles and spoons have honed my suicidal and homicidal instincts now and then. My simmering feelings of revenge, sometimes without reason, sometimes out of genuine anger, at times, out of feelings of betrayal have boiled over through experiments with knives and choppers and slicers and graters. Whenever I felt suicidal after one of those do-or-die squabbles with my husband, my temptation to kill myself would be triggered off with kitchen implements imaginatively designed by a designer who anticipated their double-role for oppressed and suppressed women. Yet, as soon as I tried to kill myself with a freshly sharpened kitchen knife, my hand shook like one suffering from Parkinson's. I let go of the knife. It dropped to the floor with a soft rankle, cunningly masking its deadly potential. I sat myself down on the tiny kitchen floor, allowed the tears to flow till the wee hours of the morning. A few minutes before the alarm went off, I went to sleep next to my husband. No one knows of my aborted attempts of suicide in the kitchen.

When she decided to leave with her husband, I hid a sigh of relief. There would be no more jostling and elbowing and crowding of two women within my private space. Two women distanced in terms of time, age, culture, background and most importantly, their respective senses of private space. She hates the kitchen and everything that goes with it. I love it. I am passionate about it. She spends most of her time at her workplace and in the privacy of her bedroom. She steps in occasionally to make a cup of tea for her husband. Or, maybe, fry an omelette for her father-in-law. On a rainy Sunday, she sometimes deep-fries onion puffs coated in gramflour batter to go with the evening tea. She even cooked an entire lunch on a holiday, vegetable fried rice that went wonderfully with boneless chilli chicken and mutton cutlets with a salad tossed in to undercut the oil and the spices. There was also a large bowl of *paayesh* for dessert. Although I hate to admit it, she did a pretty good job of it. My husband was all praise for her cooking. Which scared me somewhat. "What if she takes over completely?" I asked myself. "Whatever will I do without my kitchen?" I needn't have worried. That was the first and the last time she cooked a complete meal. "I hate cooking maa. But I wanted to show you that I am as capable of cooking a complete meal and cooking it well as I am in auditing the accounts for the firm I work in." I knew she said this on purpose to make me feel small. I did feel small. But the relief her statement brought was more important for me than my being made to feel small. My kitchen was safe.

"I'll manage maa, you don't need to help. Go watch that favourite serial," she'd say, on the rare event of her toying with cooking. I knew she was trying to feign a kindness she did not feel. But I waited at the door, afraid of this unwanted encroachment into my private space.

"I'll help you with the tea, *Boumaa*, it is Sunday, and you deserve the rest," I would tell her timidly, afraid of her response.

Then, Sumit brought the news the other day. They were moving because her husband got a promotion and a Delhi posting where the company quarters had a kitchen with much more space and air than this one. She would go subsequently because she needed to get a transfer. In the meantime, she would live with her parents, at the other end of the city. Her husband, I reminded myself, was also my son. Once upon a time, he was *only* our son. Slowly, steadily, I watched with mesmerized eyes, the son peel off the son-identity till his husband-mask merged into his face, his psyche, his persona. Till there was no son left. At rare moments, I watch the mask cracking at places when Sumit the son, unwittingly peeps out, with that smile from his boyhood days. He surfaces at the kitchen door, filling it with his tall frame like a three-dimensional photograph one sees in advertisements, and in dreams. His eyes still crinkle up at the corners and there are creases on his nose that make him look like a little boy who has just found his lost teddy bear. Then, as suddenly, the crack dissolves, the mask is back; he turns around and walks back to his room. I watch his broad, receding back. Some of the tea I am pouring out into the cups sloshes over into the saucers and I know his father will not like it. But I am past caring.

They are leaving for a new place, a new life, a New World. Just before she gets into the car, she turns around and tells me once more, with a slight hint of apology in her soft voice, "the kitchen is too small, maa." For once, I throw my submission out of the window, out into the world out there, and surprise *myself* more than others, by answering back.

"The kitchen is not small, my dear. You have grown too big to fit into the kitchen. It is *my* kitchen. It is *my* space. There is no room in it for anyone else."

# No Forwarding Address

Alice tightened the seat-belt long before the aircraft was scheduled to take off. She was one of the first passengers to have checked in. She was in a real hurry to fly back. She was aware, but indifferent, to the snobbish stares of the lady seated next to her. Can a stare be snobbish? She asked herself. One more glance in her neighbour's direction confirmed her doubts. Mrs. Hi-Funda tried to increase the distance between Alice and herself by edging on and on towards the aisle-side armrest of her seat as if she wished to dig herself into the armrest. When she saw digging herself in was not possible, she just gave up. Then she took out a sparkling white, perfumed, lace handkerchief from her Gucci handbag and covered her nose with it. Alice knew that the snub was directed at her. As usual, she ignored it.

Over the past twelve years, she had been on holiday back home to Kerala in India, just thrice. Each time, it was the same scenario, even if the character she shared the row with happened to be different. The men were a bit nicer. In the sense that they did not go out of their way to brazenly exhibit a handkerchief over a snobbish nose. At the same time, sometimes, they made a deliberate effort to squeeze their way to the toilet much too often, touching her along the aisle seat as they went. They'd graze against her, trying to get a feel of her lavish breasts. This too, did not faze her one bit. Alice was drunk with happy feelings of going home. This time, for good. She anxiously looked forward to seeing her sons and daughters back in her Kerala home, a few miles away in the suburbs of Kottayam. Some lady from back home in Kerala had won some big prize for a book she had written, Alice recalled. Her boss-lady, Mrs. Aly Khan, had told her this. She was a real nice lady, Mrs. Khan was, said Alice to herself. She had to admit that she did feel a bit sorry to leave the lady and Missy Baba behind. After all, she had entered the Khan family's service when Missy Baba was just five years old. Now, Missy Baba was 17, about to be married, with four brothers and sisters following her.

None of them, however, could compare with Alice's own brood of four—Peter, Michael, Rita and Salome. Rita was married already with two tiny tots of her own. But she lived nearby and Alice dreamt of babysitting for her daughter while Rita went off to the nursing home in the neighbourhood where she put in shift duty as an *ayah*. Salome was as old as Missy Baba herself. A bit dusky and healthy, with lovely, wide eyes set on an oval face framed with a bevy of curls. Salome worked in a beauty parlour as hairdresser. She was looking for work in Dubai because she needed money to marry her boyfriend Samuel and settle down. The boys were lovable alright, but spoilt silly by Alice and her husband, Patrick, dead for five years. Both Peter and Michael were school drop-outs and did nothing much other than actively taking part in streetside brawls and living off the rent from the portion of the house they had let out to two families. They chased girls and watched video most of the time. The only heirloom they carried in their genes was their dead father's love for the bottle. A love Alice did not bother much about because it did not surpass their love for their mother. They loved their mother much, much more than they had ever loved their father, Patrick Thomas. Being thorough Christians, they never missed Sunday mass.

Her eyes turned misty as Alice went along on her nostalgic trip to the past and the future. She took a handkerchief out of her weather-beaten leather purse, a hand-me-down from the kindly Mrs. Khan. As she wiped her eyes, she noticed that Mrs. Hi-Funda was looking at her a bit angrily, because the handkerchief Alice used was as delicate as her own. The fragrance was Poison, another hand-me-down from Mrs. Khan but since Mrs. Hi-Funda had no way of guessing how or where Alice could lay hands on Poison, she was angrier still. The rich hate to see the poor using what they use, as if there is a hierarchy in the use of expensive things like dainty handkerchiefs and branded perfumes. As if they have a monopoly over expensive things. Alice couldn't care less. She drowned herself in thoughts of the future. Or, were they really memories of the past? These days, time was too diffused, too unfocussed for Alice. The past, the present and the future telescoped into each other quite freely, sometimes confusing her more than making her happy. For instance, instead of addressing Missy Baba as Missy Baba, she would call her Salome. Maybe, because they were around the same age. Or perhaps, because she wished she was with Salome back in Kottayam than with Missy Baba in Dubai. Alice never could rid herself of feelings of guilt for having left Salome alone with her ageing mother when the girl was only five years old. Patrick, when he was young, had a girlfriend from his bachelor days to keep him company while Alice was away. Alice was hurt when she first heard of the affair. But she knew it would end one day. It did. The widowed girl, Phelomena, soon left for a Sharjah family to earn enough money to feed her brood of three, left behind with her ageing parents.

Alice picked at the food when the stewardess brought the tray in. She was too immersed in her thoughts to care about orange juice and roasted chicken. She sipped her coffee absent-mindedly, so did not notice that it was both watery as well as cold. The roasted chicken was leathery and the juice was bitter. The French fries had gone soggy and soft while the salad was too salty. The chocolate fudge dessert was tasty though, but Alice had no taste left in her mouth. Thoughts of her grownup children blended into happy moments spent with the five Aly children whose *ayah* she was for twelve long years. Rukhma, Missy Baba in other words, totally depended on Aliceamma for every little thing she misplaced, or, for a favourite dish she was looking forward to, or, to go to the gym with, which was right inside the spacious Aly home. Gone would be the luxury of a well-lit, air-conditioned room to herself with an attached bath. Gone would be those days of taking the children out for an occasional movie, or, watching a video movie with little Amir perched on her heavy, soft, lap. But these pleasures were little, or, nothing, when compared with the feelings of love that arose from within her as memories of her children wiped the others away. It was like cleaning the blackboard with a duster and beginning to write all over again.

When the public announcement system announced the landing of the aircraft at Sahara airport in Mumbai, Alice was startled out of her day-dream. The first and the biggest slice of her journey was over. She had to collect the CD-player, the computer and the microwave oven from the baggage collection point and take it through customs. Her earlier visits had brought home a sophisticated, stereophonic music system, a big-screen colour television set, an expensive camera, a ten-unit mixer-grinder, a vacuum cleaner, a juicer, the works. She had even brought money saved up from her earnings to extend the house, to have the floors mosaic-ed., and to add one floor to the single-storey bungalow. It looked beautiful from outside, what with Salome having created a nice little patch of garden with roses and things. And all this was after having sent Patrick enough money to run the house, to look after the medical expenses of her mother-in-law while she was alive, and to cover the expenses of her children's schooling. The Thomases did have some cultivable land. But Patrick had sold it all away, piece by little piece, to pay for his daily drink. Of course, all this would never have been possible had Alice not taken the decision to accept the Dubai job when she was just in her thirties. And had she depended only on the salary the Khans paid her. She had to do some extra work on the side. Such as massaging Mr. Khan on an occasional jhoomma day, the day the Muslims offer their prayers at the mosque. Or, through selling a little bit of comfort to the odd Indian immigrant who had left his wife and children behind to live all alone in faraway Dubai. They were generous, the men were, including KhanSaheb who always rewarded her with a generous tip. Alice rationalised her prostitution through her homespun logic: if the selling of comfort could buy comfort for those who were closest to her heart, then there was really nothing wrong with it. Besides, her family did not know and what they did not know, made no difference to them. She did this under the veil of going to the only church in the neighbourhood because her employers, who were Muslims, had no way of knowing that mass was mainly offered on Sundays and not on Fridays, their jhoomma day.

The domestic flight from Mumbai to Thiruvananthapuram seemed to go on and on. Firstly, the aircraft remained parked in the runway for two hours for some technical snag, which no one bothered to explain. Secondly, the in-flight staff had switched the air-conditioning off and within the sweltering heat, Alice had nothing to do but catch up on lost sleep. Being used to the heat in Dubai, this heat did not bother her one bit. Thirdly, when the plane took flight, Alice was fast asleep and had to be awoken by the stewardess who, in a brusque tone, asked her to fasten her seat belt and to raise her seat to upright position. Alice promptly went back to sleep and to her favourite pastime—dreaming.

She was an incorrigible dreamer who was equally adept at dreaming awake and dreaming in her sleep. It was a childhood trait she could not, rather, *did not* wish to rid herself of. Her dreams had made life away from home pleasant and cheerful. Her dreams were golden sunshine and liquid honey, because she never ever had nightmares. She had no idea about what they were or what they were like. Her dreams were moonshine and pattering rain, slanted pencils of sunlight filtering in through the glass-covered venetian blinds of the French windows to fall on the marbled floor of the Aly home. She dreamt colourful dreams of cuddling little Doll, her granddaughter, in her ample arms. She dreamt sound-dreams of her sons belting out loud and musical Malayalee songs around a campfire during Christmas in their backyard. She dreamt of being young all over again, revelling in being made love to by Patrick, at night, on the sands of the beach at Kovalam, which she had seen only in picture postcards and on TV. Her dreams took in the fresh whiff of an oven-fresh welcome plum cake baked by her daughters in her honour. The sweet fragrance of vanilla essence in the cake mingled with the lovely ice-cream pink colour of Doll's birthday dress she had sent from Dubai. This telescoped into another dream where Missy Baba's smiling face changed to Salome's sad face and then turned back to become Missy Baba, asking Aliceamma to tighten the belt of her gym dress. She rose to tighten the belt on Missy Baba's gym dress. As Alice turned her around to face her, she found herself looking at her own face when she was 17 and crazily in love with Patrick, six months before they had a Church marriage.

Alice did not realise she was smiling in her sleep, till the stewardess gave her a gentle nudge. She woke up to find Mrs. Hi-Funda throwing furrowed brows in her direction in the deepest frown she had ever seen. Still a bit disoriented, Alice saw they had arrived when the 'fasten-your-seat-belts' sign went up. She looked fondly out of the window to catch a small square of the India she had left behind, as the plane taxied into the runway. It was a lush green India. An India filled with her four children, the home she had lovingly built for them, a nest to come back to, like a homing pigeon. She was already getting on in years for the *jhoomma* extra-income bit. Besides, all that talk of AIDS she saw on television and in movies was enough to scare her off any intention of selling 'comfort' to homesick Indians in Dubai. Her children had all the comfort she could buy for them.

No one had come to receive her at the airport. Alice was neither disappointed nor surprised. Since Patrick died of liver schirrhossis, no one came to receive her. "The children are just too busy," she whispered to herself, as if in explanation. She knew she was consoling herself. But it did nothing to puncture her joy. She took a private taxi, reminding herself that since she had earned so much in the past twelve years, she was entitled to enjoy at least some of it. As the taxi breezed past, she caught the fields and the trees speed by. The ponds, the lakes, then the houses looming large as they made their presence felt with the taxi stepping within city limits. At a traffic light, she waved at a young mother with a baby in her arms and the woman waved right back. "It is just wonderful to be home," she kept on telling herself. Alice resisted all attempts of the driver to draw her into a tête-à-tête. She was too drunk with the joy of rediscovering her roots all over again. She tried to catch the eye of passengers in neighbouring cars as they sped past, just to flash them a welcome smile, as if trying to tell them—"are you coming home? I am coming home too." The ecstasy of homecoming was so tangible, so strong, that it made her forget all those years of living away —from her family and from her country, of putting in hard labour for years together, of depriving herself of the joys of

wifehood and motherhood, of selling the service of her body
to buy goodies for her close ones. So tangible that she felt she
could reach out and touch it.

As the taxi drove into the lane where the Thomas
bungalow stood, Alice discovered, with shock, that there was
no bungalow there. All that remained of the bungalow was the
patch of garden with a few rose bushes, drying up in rebellion
against wilful neglect. A few discarded toys of her children
when they were little were strewn here and there. Patrick's
walking stick led a lonely life in the overgrown thatch of wild
grass. The driver she had designedly avoided right through the
drive, turned out to be a sympathetic soul. He parked his car
at a safe spot, checked the lock on the car dickey, and set about
with Alice to find out. Alice knocked at the door of the Nairs,
their immediate neighbours, who lived a block away, their
bungalows separated by a small playground for children. A
maid answering the door informed them that the family was
away in Mumbai to attend the wedding of a close relative. She
knew nothing of the Thomases, she said, because she had just
joined the Nairs. She went on staring after Alice as she walked
back to the gate, her shoulders now bunched together wearily,
her gait slow and halting. Then, with a sigh, the young girl
turned in, pulling the door shut after her.

The Koshys were of no help either. The family comprised
of a doddering old couple and their very old servant, whose
memories persistently played hide-and-seek with their senses
of sight and hearing. At first, they mistook Alice for their US-
settled daughter who had promised to fetch them to take
them back to the US five years ago. But never did. When the
driver patiently explained to them who Alice was, all they did

was shake their heads in disbelief, look at each other in shock and cluck their tongues. Then, they promptly went back to their TV set and forgot all about their new visitors.

Then, they ran into 'luck'—if one could call it that, when they pressed the musical bell of the Joshys. The younger Mrs. Joshy, the daughter-in-law of the widowed old matriarch, was kind. She bade them sit, and then asked the maid to bring in refreshments of filter coffee and homemade banana chips. Alice was too impatient to savour hospitality at that moment. But politeness stopped her from refusing. Saira Joshy informed them, haltingly, bit by slow bit, that the Thomas boys had sold off their bungalow to a real estate developer. The two sons had moved away to Thiruvananthapuram, into an apartment of their own, bought off the proceeds of the bungalow sale. Rita had moved on to Doha, with a new job in a private nursing home, leaving her children behind to be looked after by her in-laws in Cochin. Salome, presently living with her brothers who refused her any share of the flat or the money that came in from the bungalow sale, was preparing to leave for Bahrain to join a beauty parlour as hairstylist. She had split with Samuel because he did not want a girl without a dowry to her name. Alice slowly made her way back to the taxi. She realised there was no home for her to come back to. Nor was there one she could *go* back to. There was no forwarding address.

# *Shoes*

You may not have noticed it, but I have a distinct limp on my left foot. It is a genetic disorder, they say. The left foot is slightly shorter than the right. Or, maybe, the right foot is slightly longer than the left! Tick the one you think is right, like the options given in a multiple-choice question. I, personally, do not care. I have absolutely no idea of what it feels like to have two identically shaped feet. I've never had them. It is as simple as that. The one that is shorter, is also a bit skinnier than the longer one. This is precisely why I love my left foot more than the right. Like a mother who has a special weakness for the weaker child in the family. She treats this child differently too. Never mind that she fiercely resists any suggestion of the same up front. I caress my foot whenever I can. I touch 'her' softly with the palm of my right hand and let it run down the leg till I reach the foot. I tend to her lovingly. I whisper sweet nothings to her when no one is looking. I've even christened her with a name. Footsy. "I love you Footsy. Because you need more loving than your twin does.

Don't mind people staring at you with intrigue. I am there to love you for keeps. I shall love you till I die." I do not realise at that moment that my favourite Footsy will die alongwith me. I use a cool massaging cream on Footsy every morning before I leave for work. I know it is of no use. But this tiny little everyday 'tribute', (I refuse to degrade it as a 'chore') to Footsy makes me feel she will not feel 'ignored' or, in whatever small way, 'abnormal.' Footsy does not quite 'answer' because she cannot speak. But she responds to my touch. She throbs right back at the points I touch her in, whenever I do. So, we, that is, my Footsy and me, have created a kind of a two-way rapport no one will understand. Footsy is fair, svelte and slim. She is beautiful, because she is not overly rounded out like her twin, my right foot.

Ever since I was born with this slender, weaker, shorter foot juxtaposed against the strong, rounded, longer one, no attempt by my parents was able to set it right. The physiotherapist, Archana Paul, who came in twice a week since I was six months old, finally told them that it would be better if they accepted this reality. "It is not as if she is totally handicapped. For all practical purposes, she is as normal as any average child is. Spare her this special treatment. It's costing you the earth and its doing no good. Either to the foot itself, or to your child's ego." The famous orthopaedic surgeon who was specially called in to take a look at Footsy and suggest a 'cure' said it was just fine to keep her the way she was. "There is no guarantee that surgery can take care of this. Besides, why make her suffer for such a minuscule disorder? The money you'd have to spend on this needless exercise would serve her better if invested in a proper, well-rounded education," he said, giving the lie to the medical profession having turned totally mercenary, commercial and opportunistic. In a manner of speaking, they were right. This 'defect', as they like to call it, generally passes notice. Because, since I began schooling, my mother taught me to wear shoes with uneven heels custom-made for me. I do not care for this, though. I genuinely believe that I am *made* differently. I enjoy the reality of the situation. I guess I was *designed* to be shaped and sculpted this way, by that person who, at times with ambivalence, at times with absolute certainty, we vest with that label 'God'.

The buzzword these days for people like me is 'physically challenged'. Frankly, I don't care for it. I don't feel physically challenged at all. In fact, I actually feel physically *gifted*. I do not understand why all 'normally' made people are convinced that we need their empathy, kindness and help. Maybe, a few of my ilk do feel the need for such 'kindness'. I, personally, don't agree. I refuse to make these so-called 'normal' people feel great by patronizing people who, they believe, are 'physically challenged'. My parents have not once taken advantage by filling in the line for *physical disabilities, if any* in any of the forms they have had to fill in on my behalf.

The gym teacher at school, Guptaji, was very strict. He'd force me to watch as the whole class did its drill or played games at the playground. "Come on, join them" he'd order me, in his booming voice that sent shivers down several spines. Sliding out of my custom-made shoes, I'd limp along to join the class at mass drill. He also made me join the March Past and the Salute on National functions like Republic Day and Independence Day. The only thing he did not force me to do, was take part in games that needed too much of footwork, like running, football, cricket, *hu-tu-tu* and so on.

When I was little, I remember my father lift my feet gently, place them on his lap, and massage them with a cool massage oil. "My little Kuchikoo" he'd say, as he'd dip his soft fingers in the ointment and apply some of the white, luminous paste to my feet. He took care to massage *both* my feet so that tending more to the 'bad' foot did not make the 'good' one weaker. He would do this only on weekends. Other days, I had to go to school and he had his work at the bank. Mother was always a bit grumpy because she had to give up a well-paying, highly challenging and creative job at an advertising agency to take up a less-paying, and much more mundane job in a school to coincide with my vacations and holidays. A 'handicapped' child could not be left alone, could she? It was just not done. She loved me deeply though. Only, I never really cared about the ways she used to show her love. "Come on, get dressed! Get going. Don't expect us to wait on you every waking minute. We have a life of our own, understand?" she'd say. And she'd go right ahead and do precisely that! Wait on me every waking minute! In all her conversations, commands, complaints, accusations directed at *me*, I loved her way of trying to be crisp and dry and fresh-smelling like a bundle of brand new hundred-rupee notes stapled and pinned on one end. I loved her for this. But, in subconscious imitation, I never let her on into this secret.

No one was really bothered about what *I* felt about my own so-called disability! All the massaging my father so lovingly practised on me, did little to 'cure' my foot. I loved this because I loved the idea of being 'different'. My parents did not understand this. They felt very bad that I could not participate in school sports. I could not run. I could only hop. Kids in the neighbourhood would use me like a 'raw lemon' (*kaccha nimboo*) for hop-skip-and-jump games. 'Raw lemon' is one who never gets 'out'. I loved the experience. My parents, I guess, were hurt. Sad rather, for an only child who could not join in outdoor sports. What the hell! I *loved* indoor games and excelled in whatever I happened to touch. Like carrom, or cards, or chess, for example. My father gave me all the practice I needed since I was a child. Perhaps, he wished to 'compensate' in some way, for my forced absence from outdoor sports. As if it was all *his* fault! Parents can really be much more naive than their own children! I took away all the prizes at school for indoor sports. My school was a co-ed one. So, for all mixed games, the boys would vie with each other to get me to partner them. I enjoyed the thrill of feeling wanted, never mind that their motivation was not often coloured by romantic notions. It was purely the 'killer instinct' in me that attracted them to me. Ironically, the same 'killer instinct' put them off when it came to dating me. Boys do not seem to care for girls with this 'killer instinct'. Even if such girls have one foot shorter than the other.

It is this 'killer instinct' that has kept me in good stead till now. Friends and relatives would vie with each other to get me to partner them in a game of contact bridge. Never mind the custom-made shoes, everyone was aware of my physical 'distortion'. You may not have noticed, but everyone is acutely observant of what *other* people's *feet* look like. Or, what kind of *footwear* they use. After looking at your face on first introduction, the eyes of a new friend will instantly shift to your feet. Besides, my shoes were special. How could anyone possibly not notice? Since nursery right until high school, I wore short-skirted uniforms, which showed off my unevenly shaped legs and those custom-made shoes—one with a high platform heel and the other with a flat one. There was really no way I or my parents could hide it from the world.

I was a ranked chess player at college and university. My mother has created a display corner for all the trophies I have won, in the living room of our small flat. Thankfully, my parents spare me the embarrassment of showing them off to guests who drop in, once again trying to underscore that though I am 'disabled' I am better at many things than those who are not! The 'compensation effect' I call it. My excelling at chess, the only sport I chose to enter competitively, took me to different parts of the country during my college days.

I carried a crush for my chess coach, Rahul Sachdev, for nearly four years. Rahul marked my debut into the 'forbidden' world of awakening sexuality. He aroused me to that hidden but very live electric current that passes between a young man and a young woman when their bodies are shaping and growing in every which way, much faster than their minds. We, I and Rahul, had a sort of an 'affair' if you can call it that. Just a bit of kissing, necking and heavy petting in dark corners of hotel rooms where we stayed, in lonely, isolated corridors when the others had left after a match, you know. Which is kindergarten stuff for today's kids fed on a nourishing diet of uncensored foreign films on satellite channels like late-night MTV shows! If you know what I mean. *Of course* you *know* what I mean! "Saami," he'd whisper into my hair, "how I love the feel, the fragrance, of your hair." I'd bury my face in his wide, wide chest, as wide as the broadsheet newspaper we read together each morning, and smile to myself. For some mysterious reason, we never once uttered those three words 'I love you' during the entire relationship. It was as if we had entered into a mutually understood, silent pact of letting them be. I did not quite believe in those words anymore since I was a teenager. They had been used, overused, misused and abused so much in literature, drama, poetry and films that, with time, they were reduced from words having meaning to mere phonetic sounds. Hollow sounds that did not mean what they intended to. Like nonsense words lisped by adults to soothe a wailing infant. "Lu lu lu, whath aal you thooing, baby?" "Will you give me a kichy kichy koo my love? If you thoo, I will buy you a thethy beal, okaay?"or something along those lines. Rahul was quite a good-looking hulk. Really. "You do make for impressive visuals as a pair, you know," said my chess-partner Vinay, a very good friend. I shrugged these comments away with a smile. But Vinay'd always say that I blushed deeply whenever Rahul was mentioned. Or around. Or both!

Rahul knew about my little Footsy. I once slid Footsy out of my custom-made shoe to show 'her' off to him. Rahul touched her softly with his fingers, his touch, featherlight strokes that made me break into goose pimples, and caressed Footsy. He slid his hand up, right up my skinny, almost bony thigh. Then, even more gently, he took his hand away. He looked deeply into my eyes and said, "It is as beautiful and soft and tender as you are, Saami." Then, he kissed me. It was a deep and long kiss. I could feel his wide chest brush against my young, full breasts. I could feel the hard bristle of the five o'clock shadow on his chin that brushed against mine. 'I was emotionally touched and sexually aroused. Decent as he was, he did not seize the moment to make love to me. I would have easily given in at that moment. I *wanted* to give in. But, he lifted his face from mine and turned away. Slowly. His movements were like a slow motion sequence in a film. Graceful, languorous, silent. I hid the sigh rising within myself, slid Footsy back into the custom-made shoe, patted my ruffled hair back to place with my healthy, shapely hands, and sat myself down on the settee of the small hotel room I shared with two other chess-playing girls from the university. I could almost hear Footsy shed unshed tears for me. By then, Rahul had left the room. So quietly, that I did not hear him leave.

Having known him for six years, I had begun to feel that Footsy's 'difference' would not deter him from elevating our relationship to bestow on it the 'respectability' marriage is *supposed* to offer. I don't know why his sudden warmth began to cool off. Maybe, it began after he once saw me whisper sweet nothings to Footsy in a hotel room during one of our trips. He must have thought me nutty. Somehow, his cooling off hurt me less than I had imagined it would! Because, then, I was more busy proving to the world out there that I was supernormal than to be hurt by a broken affair. I was too naive to appreciate that no one was bothered about any proof of my supernormality or otherwise. Looking back on those years of naivete, I now realise that I needed to prove to *myself* that I was genuinely gifted. That I could and would excel. It has kept my self-esteem intact. It has sustained me through years of struggle to join the mainstream. And yet stand out. Thanks to Footsy and my telepathic rapport with her.

Kuchikoo is not my nickname. It is a nonsense word my father has coined for me when he is in a specially caring, or, very happy mood. He does this even now, much to the chagrin of my mother who does not really care for a 35-year-old woman being called Kuchikoo by her 62-year-old father. Maa still goes about her chores, sighing all the time about my single state. Baba is not worried at all. He keeps saying, "She is as good as a son, multiplied three times over. What does she need a husband for? What she really needs is a *wife*!" Sometimes, I guess he understands me better than I understand myself. I was married once. But like all good things in life, it had to end. So, trying to evade ugly truths like all normal mothers of 'abnormal' children, Maa makes a face at him, turning the comment into a joke. I stick my tongue out at her. And this makes for a lovely, happy-family photograph for the last scene of a Hindi film.

My name is Samyukta. Saami for short. I love the feel of my full name when I am asked to pronounce it myself. The rolling of the tongue at the point where the 'm' blends into the 'y' and the 'y' is married to the 'u', then suddenly the cutting off to the hard syllables, a half 'k' and a full 'ta', has a lovely, melodious rhythm to it. My father christened me with this name. I like the shorter version as well. Specially when Baba and Maa place the stress on the 'aa' and soften the sound of the 'm'. It is pronounced *Sum-yu-ktaa*. Some mispronounce my name. In the beginning, I tried to correct them. I've given up now. Besides, most of my close friends, family members too, choose to call me Saami. "Its easier on the tongue," they say. Maybe, they are right. If I had a choice, I'd have chosen the full name.

Before we shifted to Calcutta, we lived in the ancestral Mukherjee Bari at Mewaphuli. Maa never liked it there. But she had to live there since father did not have the financial backup to set up a separate establishment in Calcutta. When Maa began to point out how the rest of the extended family stressed on my left foot, Baba started having second thoughts about staying in Mewaphuli indefinitely. "What'll happen to her? How will you ever get her married off?" Didimoni, my Baba's Pishima, would keep on cribbing to Maa, *ad infinitum*, like an old gramophone record with the pin stuck in the middle, on the same line. There was a forgotten phonograph my great grandfather had bought. You had to wind it up to get it going. It had that lovely, big brass speaker which had lost its shine over the years. The box-like contraption had carved artwork on all sides. I asked for it from Didimoni when we shifted to Calcutta. She demurred for a while, then gave in. When I was little, Baba would play old records of New Theatres' film songs on this phonograph. Songs in Bengali and Hindi sung by Kanan Devi, K.L. Saigal and Pankaj Mullick, all of them no more. I specially grew to love the *doley hriday ki naiyya* number by Kanan Devi from some film whose name I have now forgotten.

Baba has been a film buff and a film music buff all his life. He, however, cannot belt out a single note in tune. Or in rhythm. He stood out like an anomaly in the Mewaphuli home. Not if you looked at this from a totally different angle, though. Then, he was just one of a family where each member has/had his/her own obsession/fascination/eccentricity. Chhotokaka was very fond of classical Hindustani music and learnt it from a proper guru. He was gifted neither with voice nor talent. But he stuck devotedly to two hours of daily *riyaaz* early in the morning. After ten long years of struggling with the intricacies of the *tanpura*, the *harmonium* and the *tabla*, the *meer*, *gamak* and *murchhana* of an *alaap* in *malkauns*, or a Bade Ghulam Ali *thumri*, he finally managed to sing in tune. And sang rather well at that. At seventy-five, he still sings early in the morning. His voice is now slightly scarred with the brutality of time. His tune, just that wee bit off the mark. The *taal*, as good as ever, with or without the beating to time by the *tabla*. Phoolkaka and Phoolkakimaa, the handsomest ever couple Mukherjee Bari had, suffered from an abnormal obsession—their only child, Babai. The boy, a good six years older than me, was bright and intelligent. But he also had a few abnormalities as a child. Not physical, like the one I am supposed to have been born with, but other, more disturbing ones. He expressed his emotions in indefinite inertia. If he began to laugh, he'd go on laughing and no one could stop him. No one knew when and why he'd begun, and when he did, how to stop him. One of my cousins, the beautiful Pinki-didi's marriage alliance broke off because Babai-dada wouldn't stop laughing in front of the boy's family for a good one hour. They thought the Mukherjees were a nutty lot and broke off the alliance. Babai-dada was, in a strange way, sort of, addicted to water. For him, drinking water did not connote a glass, always a bucket. Several buckets, in fact. When he drank water, he closed all the doors and windows of his room, switched off the fan and all electrical fixtures if they were on, including the television, and then began to drink water from a bucket kept aside for him. The room had to be silent and he had to be left absolutely alone, to himself. He was exceptionally brilliant at studies though. But the Mewaphuli school was not good enough for him. So, Phoolkaka took a transfer to Pune and the family shifted there for keeps. They dreamt one day, he'd join the IAS. But his 'abnormal' phases disturbed his academic career. He finally managed to tuck a commerce degree under his arm, followed by a job as medical rep with a noted pharmaceutical firm. This, despite the fact that his education would often be punctuated with visits to a Calcutta nursing home for the mentally ill.

The diversion to Mewaphuli and to Babai-dada's story is because I wish to speak of my crush on Babai-dada that lasted for more than a year. Other than the crush we all had on Arindam, the rainbow-cousin, as we called him. My roots are still in Mewaphuli. Mewaphuli and the Mukherjee family have contributed quite a bit to what I am today. Both in a positive and a negative sense. I think all the female cousins slightly older than, equal to and younger than Arindam had a crush on him at some time or other. Babai-dada was tall, dark and handsome, spoke very well on any subject under the sun and belted out Rabindra Sangeet in a clear, lucid voice, without having ever taken music lessons in his life. There were several links that connected us apart from the blood ties. He was 'different' and so was I. He was an only child, suffocated with over-protection and molly-coddling. So was I. He was extremely goodlooking. So, even if I have to say this myself, am I. But time took its toll over the years and Babai-dada today, at 41, is a ghost of his former self. His wife has left him, taking along with her, their little daughter, Doll. He lives alone in the partitioned-off section of our Mewaphuli home, about to be axed by diabolic promoters. Promoters who have found an easy way to lure divided heirs to surrender to a new apartment in the newly constructed building-to-be plus a handsome account in the bank. He still drinks buckets of water with the doors and windows closed tight and the fan and electrical gadgets in the room switched off. Yet, he speaks lucidly of his ventures into writing. About how his articles keep coming back to him with unfailing regularity, with tiny rejection slips attached. About how he fails to understand what's wrong with his articles when they speak in the first person about his experiences in the mental home.

To get back to the story of Footsy and myself, we have grown together and grown too close to permit the entry of a third person singular number, masculine or feminine gender, no matter what age. This is a major reason why my brief marriage to Gautam broke up. I realised soon after, that he married me out of pity, not out of love. He caressed Footsy because he knew how much I cared for her. Then, one day, the relationship snapped, just like that. He had probably wearied of listening to my imaginary adventures with Footsy. Or, perhaps, I had realised that with Footsy, I did not really need a man by my side.

Gautam was everything Rahul was not. He was dark, square and short. He wore high-powered glasses and had bushy eyebrows. He also had a moustache I did not care for but did not mind either. I tickled it sometimes, making him laugh his loud, booming laugh that echoed happiness through the barely furnished flat we lived in. For some time during our two-year stint at playing 'marriage-marriage', he also kept a goatee. But gave it up. He dressed well and I got used to the smell of his after-shave. In many ways, without being physically 'different' like I was, he was very much like me. He took care of the antique gramophone mother gave me when we got married. He'd polish the big brass speaker with brasso every Sunday when his clinic was closed. He loved chess and that's how we'd first met at a common friend's place. He dotted his conversations with an abundance of 'thank yous' and 'sorrys' and 'excuse mes' and 'pleases'. His manner was so charming, so unassuming and so personally warm that people warmed up to him within the first ten minutes of meeting him. I was charmed too, and we got married six months after we first met.

We made wonderful, passionate, complete love every night. Sometimes, even in the afternoons when he came for lunch and stayed back for a siesta before going back to the clinic in the evenings. But sex alone cannot sustain a marriage. I had conceived once during the first year. It ended in a miscarriage and I just failed to conceive afterwards for the rest of the time we lived together. We were married, but I loved the thought that we were also 'living together'. The phrase 'living together' suited me fine because it exuded a sense of the relationship being fluid and flexible, given to change, even snapping completely. So, when we both agreed to part, the trauma was short-lived. He stayed on in the flat. It was I who returned to my parents. So, I did not have to suffer the nostalgia of sudden solitude after the partner has left. He did. I did not have to wander around in the empty flat, look at the walls bereft of the photographs that once hung there, the faded squares with the solitary nail on top reminding one of days spent in loving togetherness. He did. I did not have to prick my ears to listen to the running shower in the bathroom, waiting for him to come out after his morning wash. I did not have to roam around in the kitchen, pottering about among the pots and pans and kettles, caressing the tins and cans once filled with sugar, tea, milk powder, condiments, rice, the works that go to slowly build up a nest for two people in love, married or not. He did. Or did he? I never found out. He rang me up once in a while, to find out how I was getting along. He still does. Neither of us has found a new partner yet. But then, I don't need one. I have my Footsy. He doesn't.

On the eve of January 1, 2000, my life took a 180-degree turn. Footsy, I discovered, as the clock began to chime the bells of midnight hour on December 31, 1999, had by some strange miracle, turned absolutely, totally 'normal' and 'whole'. My own and my father's constant caring, loving, fondling, nurturing, caressing, massaging, had made her gain in what she lacked. She became rounded and whole and healthy like her twin, my other foot. I was shocked to discover that I did not need the custom-made shoe for Footsy any longer. I had to go out and buy a brand new normal pair of shoes for myself. The sudden change in my life brought forth immense possibilities. I could now do the things that were denied me because of Footsy. I could run about and play the games I never did. But I am 35, remember? And for one who has never played running and jumping games all her life, 35 is surely no age to begin. I could romp along the streets of my neighbourhood to show everyone that I no longer wore custom-made shoes. But it did not matter to me because I never was ashamed of Footsy. Footsy, I realised slowly, had changed in other ways too. She no longer responded to my touch. She did not throb back the way she used to, when I touched her at different spots along her length and breadth. She no longer 'communicated' with me like she did before, when she was 'different'.

My parents are thrilled because they can now begin boy-hunting all over again for me, if I give them the green signal. At the same time, they are shocked by my strange response to this sudden change. I am unhappy. I am desolate and depressed and lonely. I have lost my Footsy forever. I cannot bring her back to her earlier form because I wouldn't know how. Perhaps, the feeling that this 'normalcy' must make 'her' happy keeps me from trying to bring in artificial impositions of changing back. Footsy, I just know, is happy, with or without my caressing and fondling and touching and massaging. 'She' does not need it any more. Just like she does not need the custom-made shoe I have been dressing her with, for years and years and years. I have kept all the custom-made shoes I dressed Footsy with since my adulthood carefully stored in a shelf in my spacious wardrobe. Sometimes, when I open the wardrobe to set it in some semblance of order, I look at the shoes wistfully, and smile at the lovely memories of golden days gone by. There is no Footsy in my life anymore. I am a normal person with two normal feet. You may not notice it anymore, because now, both my feet are identical twins, like yours. And everybody else's.

# Subhadra's Story

Subhadra Gupta was forty-nine years old. She was already a grandmother. She had married young and had become a mother soon afterwards. Her two daughters, Roopa and Sonali, had grown-up. Roopa was already married had just delivered a chubby little boy. Sonali had completed her I.A.S. She was waiting for orders from the top about her posting. Subhadra's husband, Dr. Anil Gupta, had retired from the post of Dean of one the leading medical colleges in the city. He was in the process of setting up private practice for the first time in his life. Subhadra found, to her dismay, that she did not fit into any of the plans of her husband and two daughters. For twenty-nine years of her married life, she was busy tending and caring, fetching and carrying for others. She was happy to feel that she was wanted and indispensable. That she was loved. Some of her friends had taken up their studies some years after marriage and motherhood. Some others had taken up jobs (like teaching) that were compatible with the routined lifestyle of a housewife. Subhadra had never felt incomplete without higher education. Whatever education she had, had sufficed for tutoring the girls while they were in primary school. When they went into secondary classes, they were so bright that they did not need help at all.

So far as her husband's needs went, Subhadra was kept constantly on her toes. He depended on his wife for the smallest need from tying of his tie-knot to keeping track of his personal correspondence, including letters to his parents when they were alive. She chose and planned his wardrobe, his tour itineraries, his food, everything. She loved every minute of it. Outwardly, she did grumble within the hearing of her husband. He loved food. So Subhadra was constantly trying out new dishes, learning recipes from all over the place, till she became an excellent cook. Though later on in life, the Guptas were affluent enough to hire the services of a bawarchi, Subhadra kept tight control over the kitchen. In other words, Subhadra was the picture of a happy, complacent, fulfilled housewife. Her daughters, though, were budding feminists in the making, especially the younger one. She professed that she did not want to get married, ever. The elder one, Roopa, too, was quite liberated in the sense that she refused to give up her job as officer with a nationalised bank though her in-laws and Subhadra implored her to. Roopa's husband Sailesh, however, seconded her decision. With dismay, Subhadra watched her daughter Roopa leave her tiny one-year old with the baby-sitter. "What is the world coming to?" she thought to herself, as she filled her lazy hours watering the kitchen plants in the backyard garden.

Puran Singh, the *bawarchi*, had put in about ten years of service with the Guptas. Of late, Subhadra could feel that her entry into the kitchen was taken to be needless interference by Puran. It was her own kitchen, for God's sake! The maidservant who did the other work in the house like washing clothes, sweeping and dusting, cleaning the vessels and making the beds, also did not like to be repeatedly reminded of her daily chores by the memsahib. She knew her chores by heart. She hardly tried to conceal her annoyance when memsahib repeatedly told her to sweep the corners and under the carpet. Or, to add the correct amount of "blue" in the white bedsheets and pillowcases. She had been with the Guptas for fifteen years, what more did she need to learn? Anil, Subhadra's husband, was currently on a diet because of his hypertension. So spicy food, butter, fried food and salt were out. Subhadra thus ran out of all excuses of entering the kitchen. So far as entertaining went, Anil's medical schedule throughout his career did not leave much time for parties except when professionally called for. Informal entertaining for friends had also declined over the years principally because all their friends were no longer young and were on some kind of a diet or another.

Feeling an outsider in her own kitchen, Subhadra turned to one of her lovely talents... knitting. She knitted cardigans, mufflers, socks, sweaters, windcheaters round the year for all the members of her family including the servants. One day, however, she realized there can be too much of anything when her servants said that they had about a dozen pieces of warm clothes each and that it was time she gave them clothes for the summer and monsoon! Anil was fed up of wearing different cardigans and sweaters every day throughout the winter. He told her so one evening before stepping out for a rare walk together. "I am no longer young enough to show off a colourful winter wardrobe, Subhadra. Why don't you understand? Besides, I am a doctor and sick patients do not relish the sight of a doctor made to look as if he is dressed up to attend a fancy dress party! Doctors wear the long white coat over their usual gear for this reason." Subhadra was hurt. Anil, who had already buried his nose into the pages of medical journal, did not notice her pout. Subhadra gave up knitting. For good. She gave away her knitting paraphernalia to her maidservant Radha so that she was never tempted to knit again.

Time, however, became her worst enemy. She did not know what to do with herself. She asked Roopa to leave the toddler with her on her way to work. Roopa refused because the Guptas did not live on Roopa's route to work. Taking a detour every day meant she would either get late for work or she would have to start much earlier than she now did. Besides, "What's the need for you to slog away, mama, when I have a perfectly workable baby-sitting arrangement? Take rest now, you've slogged enough for us." "Take a holiday, go abroad, have a love affair", said her younger daughter Sonali, scandalising her mother completely. Even Anil was not to be left behind. "Why don't you join one of those kitty parties for women?" he jokingly said one day. But Subhadra could not tell them that all these were not for her. Or rather, put a bit differently, she was not for these things. How could she possibly change now? Why didn't they try to understand her loneliness, her feeling of being unwanted? Her feeling of alienation, of loss?

There was no loss. Not apparently. She had done her duty towards her family. Her daughters were fulfilled. Her husband was at last able to realise his dream of an independent practice. In a way, she had also fulfilled her material desire for a small house with a green lawn and a kitchen garden in the rear, a small car which she could drive herself, if need be, to visit her friends, or to go shopping. But was material fulfilment the only thing that made you happy? Subhadra felt she had nothing to look forward to. No waiting with baited breath for the daughters' results. No anxious hours of clock-watching when Anil was doing night surgery. His dispensary was right inside the bungalow. No counting their savings to buy a house or a car or a colour TV, video, computer. They had all these. No hunting for a marriage partner for the daughters either as one was already settled. The other had put up the "no marriage" banner high enough for everyone to read. No looking forward to holidays either as they had been to the best places all over the country. There was no place of historical interest that the Guptas had left unexplored over the years. The seaside resorts and the hill stations had all been attended to. They had even taken a trip abroad, across the European expanse after Anil's retirement and Roopa's marriage.

"Why don't you take up reading?" suggested Anil. But Subhadra had read all the classics in literature, and modern romances did not interest her one bit. These days, Subhadra found that even going through the day's newspaper took her too much of an effort. The small fonts gave her a bad headache. Nor would she go to the optician for a check-up. The video was there. But Subhadra had never been interested in films. Even when Anil sat back to catch a late-night movie, Subhadra sat next to him just to have the excuse to snuggle. She would begin to doze within a few minutes and Anil would tell her to go to sleep. Which she promptly did. Anil bought her a fish aquarium to keep her engaged. She tired of it soon after a couple of fish died. It was painful at this age to watch death, even if it happened to be the death of tiny little fish.

"It is as if it would be better for me to die now," she thought to herself. At this point of time, when she began to mutter to herself and Anil had almost decided to take her to his psychiatrist friend, an incident changed the course of Subhadra's life. It happened subtly and matter-of-factly. Subhadra realised how her life began to get rewritten much, much later. It was something as simple as Radha, her maid-servant, bringing in her five-year-old son and four-year old daughter to Subhadra to be taught English and Hindi.

"They go to a Municipal School, bibiji," she said. "They fail in English and Hindi and we cannot teach her because we are unlettered ourselves," she moaned. The children were neatly dressed. They were clean and had bathed with their hair combed back sleekly. They did not have grubby hands and feet or running noses. Radha was indeed a good mother in spite of her full-time job. But Subhadra was confused and did not know what to do. "I have not taught anyone except my own children," she told Radha. "That too, was many years ago. I have forgotten everything. I do not have the patience I had with my own girls. I was younger then. Forget it. Hire a tutor and I shall pay for him," she told Radha and turned to water the plants.

Radha would not give up though. She did not want money for a tutor. She wanted memsahib to teach her kids. No one else would do. Subhadra avoided her by pretending to be busy. Or, by running off to Roopa's house in the evenings. But the kids waited and waited for her along with their mother. One evening, returning from Roopa's house, Subhadra found the two tiny tots fast asleep on the front door steps. A chilly wind was blowing. She scolded Radha for being so negligent about the kids. Radha repeated that the kids wanted to study only with memsahib and refused to go home. Subhadra finally gave in. She took a week to think it over. What she did during this week was quite different, though. She fixed up an appointment with the optician, got her eyesight checked and got reading glasses with a new prescription. She bought herself a few books for first lessons in Hindi and English as per the current syllabus. She bought a small, rolling blackboard, a few stencils for alphabets and coloured charts. Finally, with a little hesitancy, she splashed some of her savings by investing in two small-sized school desks. She covered them in blue paint with nursery rhyme characters drawn in. All these were neatly arranged in the small room which was not in use for some time. She pulled out some old, faded, floral curtains from an old trunk and got them hung up in the small window and door of the room. It now looked like a kindergarten classroom for two students. Each morning, as soon as Anil went down to his clinic, Subhadra readied herself. Armed with book, chalks and duster, she entered her tiny "class" where her two tiny students awaited her with bright, innocent eyes, as if the mystery to the world's existence was known only to her. Soon, Radha brought the news that their school reports were definitely improving and 'teacher' was pleased. After a month or two, Puran Singh brought in his grandson Hiru, also five years old, while the gardener, who had never married, requested Subhadra to take charge of his sister's twin girls.

Within three months, Subhadra had a class of ten students between the ages of four and six. She invested some more money in desks and charts, in colour pencils and in crayons. She shifted her "class" from the tiny room to the study which was previously used by the two girls. It did not serve any concrete purpose now except for being used as a guest room now and then.

Within the span of a year, the "class" swelled to fifty students. Subhadra found that she could no longer handle it alone. So she called in her next door neighbour. Mrs. Khanna, slightly older than Subhadra herself, was a graduate, so could handle higher classes. Mrs. Khanna's joining Subhadra as a teacher proved to be a godsend for her daughter-in-law Veenu. Before Mrs. Khanna had joined Subhadra, her only occupation in life was to nag her daughter-in-law as soon as the men had left for work. Mrs. Khanna soon stopped pestering her daughter-in-law because she was too busy in the "class". Even when she came home, she was kept busy through the corrections she was burdened with. Mrs. Shrivastava, who gambled away a lot of her husband's hard-earned money on cards and rummy, joined Subhadra on the first anniversary of her "class" just to be one-up on Mrs. Khanna, her arch-enemy. But the pace and the challenge of the work in the "class" kept human frailties like enmity and one-up-manship at arms' length. Slowly, these women found their purpose in life. Their personalities changed for the better. Subhadra's life now had a new meaning. She did not charge any fee. She took the honorary services of only those women who had crossed forty-five. Nothing, she understood, was as important as fulfilling the needs of others. This self-fulfilment could be achieved through extending oneself beyond one's immediate family as Subhadra was doing now...by teaching children who cannot get such help from their own parents, or from their financial sources. Or, such self-fulfilment could also be achieved by extending oneself to utilise one's education or talent to gain economic independence as her daughter Roopa was doing. She also learnt that a working mother can be a good mother as Radha and Roopa were. That it was wrong to focus your whole existence towards attending to the basic and material needs of just your own family. That when these needs become redundant, you too, will become redundant in their lives.

Within two years of her "class", Subhadra got her institute registered as a social welfare society. She extended these classes to include unlettered women in the neighbourhood like Radha who could learn to read and write in the evenings for an hour, on weekends after the daily grind was over. That is Subhadra's story. It can be yours too.

# The Girl Who Always Smiled

On the last day, Suhasini sat on her favourite rocking chair in the ground floor verandah of their large house. She rocked herself back and forth, back and forth, as if she would never be rocking on it any more. The rocking chair was an antiquity, one of the few things in the house older than Suhasini's father. Crafted out of walnut wood, it was a hand-me-down from her great grandfather, whose oil portrait still hung on the back wall of their spacious drawing room. The colours on the portrait had faded with time, unevenly, turning his benevolent smile to an ugly grimace. Time had a cruel way of turning things around to mean exactly the opposite of what they were originally supposed to mean. The polish on the rocking chair had worn away, revealing patches of a jaundiced yellow. One of the wide armrests threatened to fall off its 'roots' so one had to sit gingerly, avoiding that side of the chair. Its cane backing and seat had gaping holes because no one had bothered to re-cane it after Suhasini herself gave up on it a few years ago. When her brothers' wives redecorated the house five years back with designer furniture, Suhasini put her otherwise nimble foot firmly down this once. She held on to this rocking chair, the dressing table with the ornate mirror in her room, and the huge four-poster double-bed her parents slept in, with the youngest child sleeping between them till he/she was big enough to move out into the children's room.

There were a few other hand-me-downs she hated to part with. The *aalna*, a typically Bengali wooden contraption to hang your everyday clothes in, a mirrored wardrobe with a carved top and an ornate, porcelain handle, and a few copper and brass pooja vessels her mother had given her. She hardly used any of these except the four-poster, the dresser and the wardrobe. They were a joke on her life and her lifestyle. She had remained single all her life so the double-bed was a luxury for her small frame. The dresser was an anomaly for one whose links with feminine cosmetics were non-existent, save for the comb and the carved-handle hairbrush she hated to part with. Her lustrous mane was the only concession Suhasini made to her vanity. But it was a secret she fiercely guarded through her life. If those brothers' wives understood, they dared not let on, at least to her face. What went on behind her back, did not bother her. The wardrobe was almost like a spacious room. Suhasini's white, cream and off-white sarees were so few that the rest of the space inside could hardly be filled with those copper and brass pooja vessels she had no use for. There were a few albums of photographs that traced the family tree of the Choudhurys back to at least two generations, after the invention of the camera, of course.

Suhasini sat rocking herself, back and forth, back and forth, oblivious to what was going on behind her. But her sensitive ears picked up sounds of packing—clothes, bags, suitcases, boxes. Sounds of folding—shelves, beds, tables, chairs. Sounds of furniture dragged across the large-tiled floors, cartons being opened, folded, closed, tied up in chords to be piled onto the waiting trucks outside brought in by Movers and Packers. The house was being handed over to some hotshot promoter to be converted into one of those horrendous skyscrapers. This house with rooms large enough to cycle around in, would soon metamorphose into small apartments with flats having tiny rooms for each nuclear family. The house had many rooms. "Too many rooms!" said her brothers in chorus, when she registered her protest against giving it over to the promoters.

"See how many rooms we have?" her mother would ask, when they were little. "One is the Happiness Room where you can go when you feel like a good cry," joked her mother. The room, devoid of light because no one had thought of replacing the fused bulb, the windows barred up with wooden crossbars, was like a large waste-bin of left-overs from a lost past. Or, perhaps, a private museum gone to pieces. Pieces of glass prisms from a fragmented and decimated chandelier, an old and darkened pooja lamp standing forlorn, in one corner, covered with the soot of forgotten oil. An ornate hat-and-coat stand with a small oval mirror her grandfather, she was told, had bought off a British officer when the latter quit India. A few oil portraits of their forefathers piled one on top of the other, in a haphazard way, in another corner. Some old gramophone records from New Theatres or Aurora or Madan Films songs they got to hear as small kids, before the gramophone was flicked by a runaway servant and no one knew what to do with the records. A large-size mirror with its mercury chipped off the Belgian glass. So when you tried to see your image in it, you could get to see collages of yourself with some pieces missing, like a badly assembled jigsaw puzzle. Suhasini took her mother's words to heart. She often used the room for a good cry after a big fight with her brothers, which she always lost, or, after having been rebuked strongly by her father for not doing well in her exams. Within ten minutes, she would come out, wiping the tears off her eyes with the hem of her frock, forgetting all about her frilled knickers showing, smiling and cheerful all over again. It was a trick that never failed. She usually lived up to the name her parents had christened her with. For she, Suhasini, was 'the girl who always smiles'.

"There is a Sadness Room as well," her mother pointed out, "you should go in there, on the attic when you are too, too happy and feel like crying a little, just for the heck of it!" Suhasini did not try this one out, ever, because the terrace gave her the creeps in the dark. Too many shadows fell across its high walls, shadows that kept moving along with the change in the glow of the street lights outside. Besides, why would one wish to feel sad when one was happy? She could never figure this one out. Her mother was really funny at times! She was terrified of shadows as a young girl. With a wistful smile, Suhasini felt that at this point of time, she was no more than a shadow of her own self. Was she scared of her own shadow?

There was the bridal room on the first floor, earmarked for all newly weds who performed their *phool sajja* (flower-decked bed) to consummate the marriage. Each one of her brothers and their wives had their *phool sajja* in this room, the large, four-poster bed decorated with a mosquito net woven out of flowers. The bride would wear floral jewels, from the crown down to wristlets, armlets, ear-rings and hair-bands, all of which the brand new bridegroom was supposed to take off, one by one, setting the right mood for a night, they said, was filled with 'romance' and 'love'. The truth is, that it only meant panic for the girl whose virginity would be ritually violated that night by the man she was married to. The room used to have several holes bored into the door by older women relatives, mainly widows, to peek through in the middle of the night, a traditional custom Suhasini did not care for. Her second sister-in-law got the holes sealed with wax and putty, because she found this socially sanctioned violation of a newly-wed's privacy disgusting! It was an exercise in futility though, because by then, all their widowed relatives had passed on. The present generation did not even know of the custom. In retrospect, Suhasini felt sorry for those aunts of hers, who, widowed when young, used this as their only vicarious enjoyment of a sex life they had been deprived of.

Her parents had their *phool sajja* in this room too, as did her grandparents before them. This room did not mean much to Suhasini however, because, being a daughter of the family, she hardly used it. Her single state denied her the opportunity of lying on this bed except on occasions like a marriage or a thread ceremony when her more spacious room was in demand for visiting relatives who dropped in for a few days.

The room they all hated as children was the Tution Room where they spent a major slice of the evening after school as the private tutors stepped in, one after the other, to teach them Maths, English, Physics, Chemistry, Biology and History.

The Maths teacher, Hari Babu, who also taught their father when he was in school, was so dodderingly old that within five minutes of his arrival, he went off into a deep sleep, after giving them some simple sums to solve. The minute he dozed off, they'd all shut their exercise books and sit down on the floor to play ludo or snakes-and-ladders. Their whispered arguments kept time with the rhythm of his loud snores in the background. Hari Babu taught them for five years and then begged to be left alone, because he had lost both his hearing and his vision. They were more than a little sorry to see him go because with the new teacher, all the fun with ludo played against a soundtrack of rhythmic snores was gone. Of the other teachers, Suhasini did not remember much. Except for the strapping young English tutor Bibhash who once tried to make a pass at her. Suhasini was thrilled to begin with. But panic followed the thrill till it became so overpowering that she took the tale to her mother. Bibhash was packed off the very next day. Suhasini would forever remember him glancing up at the large balcony to look at her before he left their house for the last time. Before their eyes met, Suhasini hid her slight frame behind a pillar. She felt a little sad because she liked him a lot. At 14, she was too young and timid to understand her own feelings.

When the house was offered to the promoter, Partho Chatterjee, it was mutually agreed that each of them, Suhasini's three brothers and Suhasini herself, was entitled to a tidy sum plus a conveniently spacious flat, once the skyscraper rose to puncture the beautiful skyline of their South Calcutta residence. "The structure is so high that you will not be able to see the sky," said a distant relative, when he heard of the change. "Nor will we be able to catch a glimpse of the green grass below," said Suhasini to herself.

They were each being given a rented apartment within a 50 km radius till the multi-storied complex was complete. Then, the Choudhurys would move right back in. "This is the best deal we could have ever dreamt of," Subhendu, the oldest of her three brothers said when Suhasini tried to voice her protest. But the chorus of three bass and three shrill voices drowned her weak resistance. She quietly retired to her room on the second floor, right below the attic on the terrace, the Sadness Room. She never stepped in there even after she grew up. She had a mental block about it. Subhendu, a year older than Suhasini and the only one she called dada, followed her upstairs to try and appease her silent anger. Like always, Suhasini resigned herself to a fate decided for her by the other six members of the family.

"It is a pity the children don't count," thought Suhasini to herself. She knew that their voices would have out-numbered that of their parents. Subhendu and Snehangshu had two children each whilst the middle one, Subhashish, had three. That made seven, ages ranging between eight and 20, plus Suhasini herself, making a total of eight. No one knew better than their Suhasini Pishima that each one of them hated the thought of leaving this spacious home to enter into a fragmented apartment where the walls would close in on them, suffocating their emotions. They hated the thought of leaving their cousins to step into separate apartments as their parents had decided, translating the emotional decimation into cruel, concrete reality. Children, noted Suhasini with a sigh, were never asked, always told. Elders took decisions, disguised as 'discussions', arbitrarily, without consulting the children. They were leaving their neighbourhood friends behind. Subhendu's wife Meena was happy with this decision. She felt the shift would nip daughter Sheena's affair with the Roys' son in the bud. Suhasini knew this would never happen because in two years time, they would be moving right back. By then, Sheena would be 20. Her feelings for the boy might, just might deepen with the forced rupture in the meetings. Besides, the flat dada and his family were moving into was just two lanes down, a distance small enough to egg on their desire to meet, yet long enough to explore alternative arrangements.

The three brothers were in varied stages of moving with their respective families into three different rented apartments, each divided more by emotional and psychological distance than by purely geographical or architectural ones. Would Suhasini be living alone? Of course she wouldn't. She was single, and a woman at that. Would her loving brothers even dream of allowing her to live all by herself at this age? Wasn't 46 a dangerous age for Bengali women of the upper middle class to be living alone? They were as vulnerable to rape and murder as was a teenager. Her brothers and their wives had drawn lots to decide who Suhasini would be living with. Suhasini resolved the problem by suggesting that she divide the year among the three brothers. She would live with each one of them for four months in a year, as did the old mother in that popular Bengali serial *Janani*. She divided the year among her four sons, living with each of them for three months, "not a day more, not a day less," decided the mother in *Janani*. Suhasini, however, did not have the kind of money *Janani* did. Nor was she privy to the dismembered, divine voice telling her what she must or must not do from across telephone lines. She did not have the kind of mafia links *Janani* impliedly had. But then, real life was different, even if one tried to 'copy' consciously or otherwise, some of those ideas in real life. Her nieces and nephews were happy to share her with their cousins. Her brothers' wives were pleased that they would not have to bear with a single, senior sister-in-law breathing down their lotioned and moisturised necks round the year. Dada was a bit sad, though, because he secretly wished Suhasini lived with his family alone. However, all this appeared rather funny to Suhasini because this was just a stop-gap arrangement. Once she had her own flat, she had announced her decision to live all by herself. And no one, not even her Dada, could make her change her mind.

Most of the things had gone with them, leaving Suhasini to supervise the packing and moving of a few last bits of furniture, much of what she had come to consider her own. Suhasini opted to monitor the last instalment of packing and moving. More because she still could not get over her mental block against leaving the home she was born in, than because she had the time and the energy to spare. Something her three busy brothers and their busier wives didn't have. Against the backdrop of a soundtrack of moving furniture, she idly glanced at remnants of the children's broken toys lying helter skelter on the verandah and the lawn in front. There was Subhojit's cricket bat, worn with over-use. It was a hand-me-down from his uncle who had managed an autograph of Kapil Dev on it. The autograph had faded with time and Subhojit had little time for cricket. He was busy preparing for his joint entrance exams. Little Sweety's broken doll, complete with her frilly pink party frock, lay in a corner, unloved, unwanted and uncared for, her eyes wide open, in surprise and confusion. With a beautiful Barbie tucked under her podgy arm, Sweety had promptly discarded the doll she had never got down to naming because it was given to her much before she had broken into baby-talk. There was a large ball made of colourful strands of wool, with the strands falling away with age. It was the only heirloom from Suhasini's craft classes in primary school, handed down from one growing nephew to the next till the ball fell victim to the vagaries of a family steadily surrendering to the temptations of an elitist lifestyle. A lifestyle created out of the legacy of prime real estate left behind by wise and thoughtful ancestors.

The screeching sound of heavy furniture dragging against the floors of the house magnified into high-decibel echoes inside Suhasini's head. She never could stand the sound of furniture being dragged across mosaic-tiled floors once tended to so caressingly by her house-proud mother. The wardrobe was already positioned in the other corner of the verandah, the wide-eyed, pink-frocked doll lying at its foot. Two huge trucks stood within the lawn, like two huge demons waiting to devour the remains of a family gone asunder under the cleverly concealed axe of modernisation and reconstruction. One by one, the four-poster bed, the *aalna*, the dresser and the wardrobe climbed into the two trucks. Each piece of furniture had been taken apart to fit into the confined space of the trucks, reminding Suhasini of a horror film showing human limbs being dismembered from bodies of people who were still alive. She requested the packers and movers to leave her rocking chair till the last. They did.

As one of the trucks backed out of the gate, another huge truck filled with the demolition squad took its place. The equipment announced its entry with sound and fury. It looked almost like a jeep at war, filled with ammunition and carbine and sophisticated firearms. The demolition crew too, was equipped like an army, uniformed, with logos on their shirts, helmet and all, as if poised for armed attack. When the packing crew came to fetch the rocking chair, Suhasini was missing. They found the chair rocking back and forth, back and forth, in inertia. Sweety's pink-frocked doll lay in it, its limbs and its head torn away from the torso, yet neatly arranged to make it appear as if it was whole. Suhasini's ornate comb and antique hairbrush on either side of the wide-eyed doll completed the bizarre collage.

They found her in the attic, the 'Sadness Room' she had never entered—as a child, or as a grown woman. She sat on the dusty floor, coiled up unto herself, rocking back and forth, back and forth, and humming to herself, snatches of some song from a lost childhood. In her hands, she clutched the large ball of colourful strands of wool. A member of the demolition squad gently lifted her by an elbow. She stood up slowly, like an obedient ten-year-old. As they walked towards the staircase, she swung an arm in the general direction of the terrace wall, saying, with an air of happy discovery, "no shadows, see? No shadows," and smiled, living up once more to the name her parents had christened her with, 'the girl who smiles forever'.

Someone with a bad sense of humour and an equally wrong sense of timing, seemed to have given the garden swing a big push. It went on swinging merrily, making a screeching noise, in rhythm—kheech, kheech-kheech, kheech, kheech-kheech, kheech—as it went up, then down, then up again in the opposite direction, defining neat semi-circles in the dusty evening air, bereft of passenger, like an eerie scene from a ghost film. Without the haunting background score.

# The Perfect Script

Like the hero in Polish filmmaker Kieslowski's first feature film, *The Camera Buff*, Rahul could not see anything without placing it in front of his imaginary camera. Camera angles and shots overshadowed his vision. He would join his palms, backside up, at the outstretched thumbs of either hand. Then, stretch out the rest of the palm straight-ahead to form three sides of an unfinished rectangle. He would then place this in front of his face, like the frame of a cinema-screen, to watch anything and everything through this 'frame'. It is a familiar pose assumed by directors and cinematographers of the tinsel world. Some directors do it reflexively; others, consciously, specially when other people, not from films, are around. Rahul did not belong to films. He did not even own a still camera, not to talk of one that took moving pictures.

He kept his ears pricked, to pick sounds off his environs, wherever, whenever. Sounds of doors being slammed, closed, shut, banged, opened. Sounds of the television remote being clicked every other second, shifting channels from the staccato

English of the BBC to the perfect Bangla of DD7 to the Mumbaiyya Hindi of ZEE to pure Urdu on the Pakistani TV and the Yankee English of CNN. Sounds of birdcalls, chirping sparrows, cawing crows, and crowing cocks. Sounds of barking dogs and mewing cats and screeching mice. Kitchen sounds of the whirring mixer-grinder, vessels being washed at the sink, a leaking tap, fish curry being seasoned in steaming hot mustard oil, starch being sieved off the cooked rice in a giant-sized sieve, the shrill shriek of the pressure cooker, his mother barking out instructions to the maid. Sound of tea being poured out of an aluminium kettle into cups, often sloshing over into saucers to make a splash. Living room sounds—of the antique standing fan, a family heirloom that made its presence felt more by the loudness of its whirr than by its speed. Or, the old radio (his father refused to give it up) blaring forth news of the day's weather in a dead monotone sans emotion or pitch. Sounds of the grandfather clock's chiming on the hour, the constant ticktock of the second's hand. Sounds of his father shuffling the pages of his newspaper, or talking to his sister in whispered tones, so that his mother wouldn't hear. Pooja-room sounds of jingling bells, jangling of keys tied to his mother's *pallu*, low-chants of mantras, blowing on the conch shell after the pooja was over, his mother washing the pooja vessels in the large basin filled with water. Bathroom sounds of the running tap, the shower in full blast from behind the closed door, the jangling of the flush chain being pulled and pulled and pulled, water gushing down the water closet, his sister belting out a Tagore song, tunelessly as usual, during a leisurely bath, clothes being washed and rinsed and beaten even when they defiantly refuse to 'die'. Day sounds and afternoon sounds and night sounds. Interior sounds within the apartment and 'outdoor' sounds from the immediate neighbourhood—the sound of a neighbour's car being parked inside the garage under their flat, his brother wheeling in his Hero Honda onto the parking lot outside the apartment block, the sound of the neighbour's daughter practising *sa-re-ga-ma* on the harmonium—something he picked up from a Ray film long ago, or the couple next door forever squabbling in voices that grew louder by the minute, indifferent to their breach of their own privacy. Sometimes, the strains of a beggar song floating in from the street outside, or the whimpering of a tantrum-throwing child followed by a few stinging slaps from his mother. He associated the smells to go with the sounds because he did not quite know how to 'store' smells. Like he still had not discovered the secret of storing 'silence'. He stored what he could, in the hard disk of his memory. To be drawn from and drawn upon, when the time came to make his dream film. He did not own a cassette recorder, much less a computer.

Rahul was jobless by choice. No amount of cajoling, begging, scolding or insulting by father, older brother, younger sister, could shake him off his obsession. He wanted to make the best film ever made. His friends had reduced him to a living joke. He had lost three wonderful girlfriends one after the other, in quick succession. They found his looking at them through that unfinished rectangle of his palms insulting and humiliating. Especially in a public place like a restaurant or a park or in the lounge of a theatre. Onlookers would watch for a minute, assume puzzled expressions and go along with what they were at. They probably dismissed him for a crackpot.

Rahul knew he was not one. He had a dream like everyone did. Only, his dream was too big, too incredulous, too much of a fantasy for others to accept and adapt themselves to.

He wanted to go to the Film Institute in Pune after his graduation. His father would not hear of it. "We cannot afford it," he said, with more firmness than he actually felt. "I am going to retire in a couple of years. You had better pull up your socks and queue up at the employment agency for a decent job. We do not have anyone in the family in films. I do not want to begin with you," his father said. Then, as usual, he hid behind the day's newspaper, a regular escape strategy from disturbing family debates he did not know how to get out of. He did not like to argue with his younger son. It always led to raised voices, angering Rahul's mother. She was far from the *sati-savitri* type. She was perfectly capable of walking out of the kitchen to go to the Ramakrishna Mission at Gol Park and listen to devotional speeches and songs. The family then had to make do with just dal-rice for lunch because Rahul's sister went to work. Rahul's father hated dal-rice. Besides, it turned the fresh, sweet-water fish he had bought from the market that very morning, tasteless and insipid within the coldness of the refrigerator's freezing compartment. It happened too often, though, because, like all Bengali families, they argued all too often. His wife, uncharacteristically named Sita by her parents, pampered and spoilt her kid son and did not care for others rebuking her favourite boy. "There is more of Hitler in you than Sita," he often told her, without result. With the solid backing of his mother, Rahul did not bother to queue up at the employment agency. He did not bother to respond to ads in the classified columns of newspapers either.

He knew he was born to make the greatest and the best film ever. A clerical post in a bank or peddling insurance or writing accounts was not up his street.

Rikta, his last girlfriend, told him to meet the great director Satyajit Ray. This would give him ideas on how to go about realising his dream, she added. So, one fine morning, Rahul climbed into the underground metro from Tollygunje, got off at Rabindra Sadan, took the rear exit, and ambled in his leisurely fashion, towards 1/1A Bishop Lefroy Road, where the great director lived with wife Bijoya and son Sandip. Ray's official photographer, Hirak Sen tipped him about catching Ray in the morning. "It is the best time to catch Ray in an ideal mood," he had said. Rahul discovered that there was a personal elevator that took one directly into Ray's living room. But the watchman wouldn't let Rahul use it. Determined to fulfil his mission of meeting the great genius, Rahul took the stairs. He was unaware of the fact that visitors who took the elevator were automatically given 'clearance' to meet Ray. Those who took the stairs, were 'eliminated'. So, when the servant who answered the doorbell would not even accept his visiting card, Rahul brushed him aside with one shove of his strong shoulder and walked straight into Ray's living room. The Nepali servant, now stacked against one of the walls of the narrow passage, gaped at this unexpected dismissal. Rahul turned back once to register how well this scene would turn if kept as a 'freezeshot' in his dream film. He'd add it to his script, he decided.

Rahul was speechless when he stepped into the room. The august presence of one of the greatest filmmakers in the history of world cinema seemed to rob him of the power of speech. There was the great master, Satyajit Ray himself, relaxed in his arm chair, pipe sticking out of his mouth, sketchpad resting on his knees folded up to make a 'table', sketching on the sketchpad. Slivers of sunlight filtered in through the slats of the large window behind him, lighting up one side of his face, adding to the sculpted features, rough, uneven, dusky, and strong. The 'picture' was a live 'translation' of one of the thousands of photographs of the great master, photographer Nemai Ghosh had taken. Ray did not notice Rahul's entry, so deeply absorbed was he in his work. Rahul was tempted to put up his palms and form his 'camera' rectangle. So before his hands rose in reflex, he shoved them determinedly into his pockets, and glanced around the room to divert attention. He realised that the left pocket of his trousers had a hole in it and a couple of fingers of his left hand stuck out, thankfully, beyond vision. He turned his mind away from those disturbing fingers and allowed his attention to wander across the room. The walls were lined with books, books and more books. There was the historic piano, its lid invitingly open, the keyboard on display, on one side of the spacious room, where Ray created many a hypnotic musical score for his later films. A book of musical notations rested on the 'holder' above. Rahul looked here and there for those famous visual scripts of Ray written and sketched directly into grocer's accounting books bound in red cloth. But they were nowhere to be seen. Rahul simulated a gentle cough to attract attention. Ray bent his head to look up at him from the top of his glasses, waved his pipe at Rahul first, and then at the circular cane stool in front of him. "Boshun," ("sit down") said the great master in his golden baritone.

Voice touched with a slight tremor of nervousness Rahul never imagined he was capable of, he told Ray about his dream. Ray put down his charcoal pencil and listened to him patiently, as he puffed into his pipe from time to time. Rahul watched mesmerised, as smoke rose from the pipe in ambivalent circles, slowly fading away and out of the large window. The fingers sticking out of his torn pocket began to twitch, reflexively. When Rahul finished, Ray asked him to show the script he had written for his dream-film. Rahul could not. He did not have one. With the rather funny confidence Rahul had acquired over time, he said, "I don't have a script, Sir. It's all written inside my head." The great director gently suggested Rahul put down in Black-and-White the script that he had in his head. "You come back and show me the script after you are finished. I'll take a look," said Ray and went back to his sketchpad, as if the dialogue with Rahul had never happened.

Mridul Sen, another famous director, dismissed Rahul almost as soon as he met the director at his modest apartment near Hazra Road. Defining a vague arc in the air with his black pipe, a habit he had picked up in unconscious imitation of his one and only rival, Ray, Sen refused to listen to Rahul's dream of a dream film. He laughed at Rahul. His cronies who had come in for a cuppa, laughed along with him. "Where's the script, my dear boy, where's the script?" he kept on asking, sounding like an ancient 78 r.p.m. gramophone record with the pin always stuck on the same line. Then, he turned to the human cutlery assembled around him and said, "this boy wants to make a great film and he does not even have a script, does not even have a script." They laughed in chorus. An insulted Rahul made his way out, slowly, silently. The only sound that marked his ignominious exit was the click of the latch as he pulled the door close behind him against the soundtrack of chorused laughter, now partitioned off by the closed door. Unknown to him, Rahul's body language had altered. His hunched shoulders and tired gait reminded one of Arnold Schwarzenegger in *True Lies*. Of the scene where after overhearing his wife, he thinks she is having an affair because he has been neglecting her.

So drowned was Rahul in his thoughts, that he failed to notice a Cielo come rushing onto him. His dream may have got crushed under the car along with him. The driver, however, was more alert. She braked the car with a loud screech. Then, stepped out, trying to help him up. She gave him more than just a piece of her mind. "What are you doing, you rascal? I don't mind one bit about your desire to commit suicide. But must you pick my car to be run under? Please, I've got a career and family to think of. Don't be so bloody selfish, you rag!" Before Rahul could open his mouth in protest, he found himself being pushed into the backseat of her lovely Cielo. He noticed that a crowd had begun to gather around them. Before it could surround the car, she sped away quickly, taking him along to her spanking apartment at Mandeville Gardens.

Who do you think she was? Hers was a beautiful face, but Rahul did not recognise it. He felt there was something vaguely familiar about the way she threw back her head to shake off the mane of lustrous black hair, the curve of her full mouth, the curls neatly arranged around her forehead to conceal its broadness. But he could not put a name to the face. She was no ordinary woman. Her name was Sreelekha Sengupta. She was currently the best box office draw of commercial Bengali cinema. Rahul never saw Bengali commercial films. He did not know one star from another and wouldn't know how to begin. Mainstream films, for Rahul, especially in his own mother tongue, were just so much wastage of precious raw stock, finely honed technical skill, and time. As they chatted over a cup of Espresso coffee she poured out of her imported Espresso machine into dainty cups of bone china, she told Rahul about herself, and about her dream. Rahul realised why her face was so familiar. It stared out of every other big-sized hoarding in the city at every street corner. The kiosks were flush with her face in close-up, wearing a different expression each time, at times, weeping away, at others, flashing a perfect set of teeth, or, in open-mouthed invitation to suggestive seduction. Rahul only saw the face, but did not care to read the credits. The face, then, meant nothing to him. Because the only Bengali films he saw were the ones made by Ray or Sen or Buddhadev Dasgupta, Gautam Ghose, Aparna Sen or Raja Mitra. He did not recall having seen her in any of their films.

"You've got to have a dream," said Sreelekha to Rahul, bringing him back to the present. She was quoting from memory, her lines from the latest film she was shooting for. "When you lose your dream, you die," she went on. Rahul, a voracious reader, knew at once that she was quoting from *A Story of Rose*. He put in his own contribution by adding one more line—"We have so many people walking around who are dead and don't even know it," he finished, hiding his pride with a deep red blush, which however, revealed more than it concealed. Sreelekha was amazed. How did he know her lines? When Rahul told her, she realised that her lines had been plagiarised by the dialogue writer and she didn't even know. This did nothing to embarrass her of course. So, she did not blush. One of the first lessons of stardom was never to be embarrassed by anything at any time. It was a lesson painfully learnt, and easily remembered. Having spent a good seven years in the film line, Sreelekha's peaches-and-cream skin was not half as delicate and as fragile as it appeared on screen.

Sreelekha wanted to act in the best and the greatest film ever made, she told Rahul. She wanted to surpass Kate Winslet in *The Titanic*, Susan Sarandon in *Step Mom*, Marilyn Monroe in *The Seven Year Itch* and Sophia Loren in *Two Women*. But no director was prepared to listen to her. All they wanted was a fat wad of currency notes pressed into their palms before discussion could begin. They wanted to discuss the 'script' in rooms booked at lavish five-star hotels with the food and drinks of course, thrown *in gratis*. She did not tell Rahul about the other side of the bargain she was not prepared to submit to. Quite a few wanted to sleep with her. Being a star, she had a very different set of morals from mainstream people. But she was no longer at a stage where sleeping around was mandatory for any and every role. Besides, she had had her quota filled and was not ready to take in any more. "Why don't you produce your own film with your own money?" Rahul asked her, though he had heard stories of the shark-like qualities star-families acquired as one of them hit stardust.

"I don't have any," she confessed. Her family took it all away, she added. In exchange, they let her live in this flat. "See this beautiful flat? My parents bought it for me and furnished it for me too, appointing Fareeda Khan to do the decor. You know, she flew all the way from Mumbai to Cal to do up my apartment and my parents paid for her ticket. Can you imagine?" she said proudly, waving her graceful arm in a liquid line to embrace the room. The walls had large-size photographs of Sreelekha in different poses. Some in black-and-white, many in colour. The black-and-white ones, Rahul noticed, were shot with diffused lenses, with careful backlighting that created an ethereal halo around the head, investing it with the star-like quality of the unreal. The counterpanes and glass cabinets were filled with statuettes and medallions of all sizes and makes, inscribed with her name, awards collected by Sreelekha for her roles in different films. One of them, Rahul noticed, was the BFJA (Bengal Film Journalists Association) Best Actress of the Year trophy. And he did not even know her from her face!

Rahul did not know who Fareeda Khan was and why her name had to be so familiar. But for him, the dazzling decor was a bit unnerving. There were imitation chandeliers crafted out of fibreglass hanging from a false plaster-of-paris carved ceiling juxtaposed against textile lampshades bought off Cottage Crafts. Priceless crystal clashed with blue pottery from Rajasthan. A batik panel on pure silk was placed right beside a reproduction of a Picasso 'blue' abstract. A brass statuette of the Buddha stood alongside a Chinese Laughing Buddha in jade, arms raised in laughter. The velvet covered settee had a stained glass center table and kantha-embroidered cushions. Rahul winced at this *pot-pourri* and mishmash decor which must have taken a neat packet out of Sreelekha's hard-earned money. "I'll never use this kind of décor for the interior shots of my dream film," he told himself.

He vaguely guessed out of sheer common sense that this flat, and everything that went into it, was bought off Sreelekha's sole earnings, as was the Cielo they had driven in. "They give me a monthly allowance that is quite generous, you know," she informed Rahul innocently. He did not care to ask her why she lived alone, and away from family. "Heroines may have their own standards," he felt. After coffee, she offered him a Scotch-on-the-rocks from the well-stocked bar. Rahul graciously refused the drink. All these years, in his determination to break every rule in the film director's book of values, he had rigidly kept himself away from the three well-known vices of filmdom—cigarette, wine and women. His girlfriends were simple friendships wrongly labelled 'affairs'. "I did not even kiss them," he said to himself, a bit remorseful in retrospect, for never even having made the attempt. He knew the girls would not have stood the test of time, dream film or no dream film. With a shock he realized, that with all his unconventional and radical dreams, he was still a virgin!

After a few more meetings, now secret by design, between Sreelekha, the star-actress, and Rahul, the would-be director of his dream-film, unknown to Sreelekha's parents, producers and gossip-writers, (since Sreelekha lived alone and only had part-time help coming in,) Rahul decided to rewrite the script of his life. He did not have to put pen to paper. He did not have to approach Ray to show him the script. Nor did Sreelekha have to ask for money from her parents to produce her own film. The two incorrigible dreamers just put their lovely little heads together to make the best film ever made. What's more, it was a 'live' film, the first such film ever made in the history of cinema. It needed no re-takes, no editing, no cinematography. No studios, no sound-rooms, no recording studios, no dubbing. Yet, the dialogues were real, springing forth naturally out of impulse, no mouthing of absurdity or melodrama written down in premeditated calculation. No wipes, no fades, no mixes, no superimpositions. No jump-cuts and no match-cuttings. No flashbacks. No montages. Nor did it need the jugglery between financier and producer, distributor and exhibitor. No promos, no PR work either. All it needed was a bit of careful planning, choice of proper 'location' and a lot of post-production work in a 'lab' commonly called 'home'.

In case you've not guessed it yet, Rahul and Sreelekha got married. They shifted to the relative anonymity of Bolpur, the picturesque little town where Tagore built his dream Visva Bharati, the University at Santiniketan, in Birbhum district of West Bengal, a 'location' ideally suited to the lifestyle they chose and the ideology they lived for—dreaming forever. They bought themselves a lovely little bungalow with the money the sale of the Mandeville apartment brought them. 'Post-production' work consisted of two little children named Satyajit and Shabana, after Satyajit Ray and Shabana Azmi, 'created' with love, in that 'lab' called their bedroom, during night shootings. This was the dream-film they opted for, when the other one did not seem to be very functional. The best and the greatest film ever made. The perfect script ever written, or rather, not written.

How do they manage to make a living? Through Sreelekha's contacts she had never exploited till then, they have built an empire in the underground hoarding and selling of cinema tickets of Hindi films in the black-market in Calcutta. They have thus created an avenue of employment for street urchins and runaways into Calcutta, conveniently distanced from direct contact with Rahul and Sreelekha and their two growing children, studying at elementary school at Visva Bharati. The Cielo is still there. They have retained it as a tribute to the memory of that first meeting. It draws a lot of public attention in this small-town. But they know that with time, the locals will get used to it. Rahul will never rush into it absent-mindedly ever again. Because he drives it himself. You do not really need to drive around much in a small-town like Bolpur. He drives it on his weekly drives to Calcutta and back, sometimes with Sreelekha and the kids, mostly alone. His hands are now conditioned to be around the steering wheel of the plush Cielo. They no longer rise, either in reflex, or by designed intent, to make that three-sided rectangle with outstretched palms to simulate the frame of a shot, viewed through a movie camera.

# The Rainbow-Chasers

Arindam's first glimpse of a rainbow was a fleeting one. From within the square window of a speeding train. Just before the sky broke out into tiny, flower-like showers. He ran to the next window, as the train sped away, leaving the rainbow behind, like a newly-crowned king proudly rising over the lush green mantle of enchantment around it. It rose regally, above the hills and valleys across the horizon, till Arindam could see it no more. The train had turned at the next curve to step into the frightening blackness of a long tunnel. The lights inside the bogey went up, but the sound of the train's wheels changed, infusing a mysterious silence among the commuters, wearily waiting to reach their destination. He was seven then. He watched mesmerised as the luminescence of the seven colours, the fine bow severed by the bars of the train window washed over his boyish, bony frame. The vision took root in his mind, like the seed of a plant. It grew slowly into a sapling, nourished with the dreams of naivete, watered generously with the fantasy of innocence, and tended to with the love and care of an only-lonely child. The sapling grew into a healthy and beautiful tree. Its trunk and branches were strawberry-ice cream pink, its leaves were a beautiful peacock blue and it sprung flowers in the seven soft-focus, luminescent colours of the rainbow. This vision slowly overpowered his thoughts, ruling them, controlling them, at times, even dictating them.

Often, Arindam would close his eyes and create his own rainbow, painting in the in-between colours that WereNotThere in the rainbow he had seen from the window of that speeding train. The purples and the mauves, those shades of blue—sky, cobalt, royal blue...the greens like olive, lemon, parrot, leaf, emerald, and the infinite hues of yellow found in ochre, chrome, buttercup, the works, defined Arindam's very own collection of rainbows. Crimsons, pinks, magentas and scarlet, coloured his imagination. He abandoned himself to this free play of his fantasy as and when he could. By the time he grew up, he had concocted an enviable database of rainbows, in all hues and colours. He tried to imagine them linear or circular, but his vivid sense of fantasy could never bring itself to defy the beauty of the liquid, lavish arc.

In his dreams, Arindam often found himself walking right into a rainbow, the colours caressing him, fondling him, enveloping him with their love from all sides. He emerged from the cotton-candy crowd of colours, his wet, matted hair dripping with droplets of rain, his wet clothing stuck to his small body. Perhaps, as the logical extension of this fascination, Arindam grew to be a painter. Interestingly though, he sketched and painted in black-and-white. He avoided colours, as if afraid of being trapped and overpowered by their strength. In course of time, his love for black-and-white almost matched his obsession for the rainbow. This evolved into a love for cinema. Old classics, Guru Dutt films cinematographed brilliantly by Murthy in black-and-white. The old films of Satyajit Ray, with aesthetically designed camerawork by the likes of Subroto Mitra. Raj Kapoor films starring Nargis with the luminiscent halo around her beautiful head, lip-synching to the tunes of a lilting song penned by Shailendra and composed by Shankar-Jaikishen. He joined a film club in course of time, taking in the magic of Kurasawa, imbibing the rich tapestry of a Bergman, amazed by the satire of Charlie Chaplin and left gaping at the enthralling suspense woven into cinemagic by the immortal Alfred Hitchcock. The cine-club reintroduced him to Kaberi, who he had first met at his art exhibition a few months before.

Arindam's first glimpse of Kaberi therefore, was more destiny than accident. There was no design in Kaberi's sudden visit to the Jehangir Art Gallery where Arindam's works formed part of a group show, his first exhibition yet. His black-and-white sketches did remind her of R.K.Laxman's crows to begin with, but as she ambled along, she was fascinated with a definite stamp of an individual style, slowly making its presence felt. His strokes were bold and strong, his idea, revolving around train windows and rainbows framed in those squares, all done in black-and-white, took Kaberi by surprise. She had just completed her post-grad in film direction from the Film and Television Institute in Pune and had completed her diploma film in black-and-white, with great difficulty because raw stock in B&W was really difficult to come by.

Adoor Gopalakrishnan, then-Director of the FTII, helped her out because he too, loved to work in B&W.

Kaberi and Arindam were drawn to each other more by their love for colour and B & W than by each other, *per se*. But the relationship grew over time, as the two struggled, in their own different ways, to come to terms with the nitty-gritty of life. Kaberi was very fond of wearing B&W which blended perfectly with her own colourful personality. Her wavy hair was brown, because she streaked and tinted it regularly. It matched the colour of her brown eyes. She was slim and svelte and tall, taller than Arindam whose lack of height did not deter her as they strided the streets of Mumbai together after sunset. Her eyelashes were long enough to cast shadows on her fair cheeks. Her full lips were so red that she never needed lipstick. She permitted herself the indulgence of mascara though, since it lent richness to those never-ending lashes of hers. Arindam was dark himself, and his complexion juxtaposed against Kaberi's peaches-and-cream had somehow invested their togetherness with a poetic justice rarely backed by reality. Arindam loved to pinch her cheeks to make them turn pink, and to hide his face in her thick hair, whenever they could manage to snatch a few moments of intimacy.

Somewhere along the way, though, Arindam's obsession for the rainbow did not match the B&W rawness of real life. His fame as an artist of promise went out when critics who panned his works strongly commented on his lack of growth. They accused him squarely of shying away from colours because he did "not know how to handle them." His clients moved over to more innovative artists who dared to experiment with mirrors and glass and frames and abstractions. Arindam called it 'commercial compromise' but Kaberi called it 'boldly innovative'. The rainbow from the train window began to chase his dreams all over again. The pragmatic Kaberi made the necessary switch to colours as she stepped into directing her first, full-length feature film. Kaberi still loved Arindam. But she was more in love with her challenging work. Her dream, unlike Arindam's, was not overpowered by colours. She dreamt of her film being screened at the Cannes one day. In the meanwhile, the totally unambitious Arindam frittered away his time neatly collecting clippings of Kaberi's progress and filing them in a portfolio. He framed the clippings with his own ornamentation, in all the hues of the rainbow. He also wrote letters to Kaberi wherever she was at a given time, in rainbow coloured stationery he designed specially for her. He managed to keep body and soul together with the rent from the house his father had left behind and from off-and-on commissions from calendar manufacturers and old photo studios which called on his services to touch up their B&W photographs with a little colour.

In his total loneliness, the rainbow colours became his closest friends. Red, his favourite, caressed his forehead when he retired for the night. "Why don't you use me in your drawings and paintings, Aru?" she asked. "Just see what magic I can do for you," she added. Indigo was a bit angry for the casual indifference Arindam revealed through his art, through his absolute monopoly of B&W. Indigo stepped in to wave an arrogant 'hello', leaving Arindam to pine in agony for a fast-disappearing friend. Blue was cool. She rationalised Arindam's sudden love for B&W by ascribing it to 'the spontaneity of human nature' and went back to her original habitat—the sky.

Green was jealous as usual. She envied Red and Kaberi with equal vengeance. She loved Arindam to a fault though. She saved him from sadness by filling his life with the lush green mantle of enchantment, shaping herself into ways of expression through the bedspread, the upholstery, the curtains, the pillowcovers and the patchwork quilt that defined the decor in Arindam's lonely bedroom. But Arindam never looked after them well. Over time, the rich green shades were veiled with thick layers of dust and grime, crying for a wash that never happened. Violet and Yellow and Orange were silent watchers who remained content guarding their lover from a distance.

While Arindam's life vacillated emptily between his awesome obsession for the rainbow and his fascination for Black & White, Kaberi made the essential and sensible transition from documentaries to feature films, from B&W to colour, from Indian film festivals at Trivandrum, Calcutta and Delhi to London, Toronto, Chicago, Berlin and finally, the Cannes. She kept track of Arindam through his letters but responded infrequently through care-of faxes and e-mails. Many of which did not reach him at all. They had drifted apart. But were yet together, by virtue of the fact that Kaberi did not have a new man in her life. Arindam did not bother to look beyond his colours and his B&W and his slow but sure distancing from Kaberi.

Kaberi's film finally reached the Cannes in 2000 AD the beginning of the Millennium. She desperately wished to share these cherished moments with the only close friend she had—Arindam. But he was recuperating from some mysterious illness in faraway Mumbai, an illness that defied both diagnosis and treatment, an illness that rendered him numb to smell and taste and touch. The only senses that remained with him were those of sight and sound. He switched on the television set in his bedroom to watch the coverage of the Cannes by some satellite channel. "They'll show you clippings from my film, so remember to stay tuned," said Kaberi's urgent Fax message delivered last night by a conscientious common friend. The clippings began, disturbed by the clipped voice of the commentator on the soundtrack of the channel. As he watched the closing shots of Kaberi's film, Arindam sat up to see himself on the small screen, walking slowly along the railway tracks to disappear into the pitch black darkness of a tunnel. His back was turned to the camera. As he watched his figure disappear after a point, Kaberi's camera drew back to move and focus on the sky. It proudly displayed the graceful arc of a brightly coloured rainbow. As the camera went into the final freeze, Arindam felt himself disappearing into the darkest tunnel he had ever seen, right there on his unwashed, uncleaned, unmade bed. His last glimpse of the rainbow was as fleeting as was the first, a momentary glimpse of the seven colours broken into separate entities, all as close to Arindam as if they would blend into him. He felt himself zigzagging his way through the railway tracks and into the tunnel. He felt the rainbow colours cry out his name, with a passion uncommon in humans, asking him to turn back just one last time, asking him to stay on in the world of colours, and light, and black and white. But Arindam did not turn back. The colours had no way of knowing that, by then, he had lost his sense of hearing. Incidentally, the name of Kaberi's film was *The Rainbow in Black-and-White*.

# The Unfinished Story

The problem with Hritwik was that he could never finish any story that he began. This is a common problem. At some point or another, we all fancy ourselves winning the Booker Prize for our creativity with the pen. Or, at least the Commonwealth First Novel Prize. Or, the Hawthornden Poetry Prize if you wish. Or, like Jhumpa Lahiri, the Pulitzer Prize for fiction or the Pen-Hemingway Short Story Prize. Never mind that some of us have a love-hate relationship with pen and paper. A few are definitely allergic to two of the most creative inventions of mankind. That does not stop us from fantasising. All of us go through a phase of poetry at least once in our lifetime. Sometimes, it is when one believes one has fallen in love for the first time, during adolescence. A personal tragedy could act as a trigger, a coping mechanism of defence. Thankfully, the phase is a fleeting one. It comes and goes like a whiff of fresh breeze floating through a sea-facing bay window to kiss one's face and go floating away. Like a lash-come-loose off your eyelashes. You pick it up gingerly, blow on it and let it fly away, after making a wish you *hope* will come true, but *know* will not. At others, a big fight with the boss, or the spouse, or a parent, or a close friend, could become the motivation and the starting point of a story.

Shirsendu Mukhopadhyay, the noted Bengali novelist, for instance, began a story about a man losing his grip on the rope he held to draw water from the well for his daily bath one morning, which aroused in him, the fear of an untimely death. Shirsendu turned this tiny event into a beautiful novel, spreading its roots and branches to span characters, incidents and events in the lives of dozens of characters. It ended with the man's suicide, an ironical climax for a novel which began with his fear of dying. Vikram Seth for instance, drew his inspiration for one of the biggest bestsellers of modern times from the everyday happening of a woman looking out for 'a suitable boy' for her marriageable daughter. Manju Kapur began her prize-winning first-novel, *Difficult Daughters*, with the cremation of her mother at the burning ghat.

Hritwik's case was different. His language was like liquid sunshine. His choice of words was painterly in its visual design. His point-of-view offered sounds and pictures that were the dreams of great writers. And filmmakers. His ideas and conceptions too, were original, exclusive, unique. What went against him were the *characters* he created. They went out of control soon after he infused them with flesh and blood. He might have quit one set of characters to get on with the next. But no. That was just not possible. Because, though they left their own *story*, they became a part of the orbit of the daydreams he lived in. They freely telescoped into his other stories, half-done, or just begun, or about to end, but unfinished, because *those* characters too, were out of control. They defined an inseparable part of his life, his mindset, his psyche. They circled him, chased him, haunted him. They stalked him at his place of work. They hovered like shadows around him. Tall and short shadows, crooked and straight shadows, male, female and child shadows, fat and thin shadows, clever and dull shadows, singing and dancing shadows, Indian and Chinese and African and American shadows. Boss and secretary shadows. They moved silently, in slow motion, in silhouette, often changing shape according to the degree and the quality of the light around them. Slivers of sunlight would cut the shadows into long ribbons of black or grey when it was day. Droplets of rain would pour off them when it rained. They reminded Hritwik of the ghosts in Satyajit Ray's fantasy film, *Goopy Gyne Bagha Byne*. They teased and taunted him endlessly. They drove him crazy with their defiance and their rebellion. Yet, they slipped away like small ice-cubes wrenched out of the ice-tray and placed in the cup of an eager palm—cold, hostile and slippery, the minute he felt he had them within his grasp. You may begin to think these characters were all in their teens. They were not.

Shyamalendu Choudhury, a Hritwik creation, in a story tentatively titled *The Ash-tray*, was 54. CEO of a multi-national corporate house, he was busy, efficient, eccentric. He kept with the times by grooming himself with a fortnightly haircut and styling at a men's hairdressing parlour. He wore the most expensive aftershave in the market and kept his wardrobe stacked with the latest formal suits, casuals, and even a pair of Ruff-and-Tuff for the occasional picnic he joined in. He wore moulded spectacles with a transparent frame.

This added to his looks. Also, to the dignity of his status. He was an accredited member of one of the most prestigious clubs in the city. This club had a gym and Shyamalendu frequented this without break three times a week to take care of his tummy which tended to go out of control. Each morning, he went to the nearest Laughing Club to keep his hypertension in control. He read *Time* and *Newsweek* and *Life* because he felt Indian glossies did not fill readers like him with details of international lifestyles. He was extremely techno-savvy and kept up with the rapid changes in infotech by upgrading the software in his office from time to time. He was a vegetarian though, and did not care for alcohol. The only concession he made to any known human 'vice' was the cigarette. He was addicted to Lady Nicotine and smoked like a chimney, never mind the smiling warnings his gym teacher threw at him now and then. His wife had given up on him so far as smoking went. Shyamalendu fit neatly into the cliched description of a typical Mills & Boons hero. But his age was in the way. Even so, those streaks of silver in his carefully styled hair did draw repeat glances from women who saw him for the first time.

Unknown to his colleagues and subordinates, behind the veneer of his suave and sophisticated persona, his three-piece suit in charcoal black, tailored at Charagh Din, Shyamalendu hid a strange eccentricity. Or, *thought* he did. Somewhere along the line, he had made a habit of collecting all the ash from the ashtray in his air-conditioned cabin to carefully pour it out into brownpaper bags. He did not know when this habit grew on him or why. Neither did he question the mystique behind it. He carried these brownpaper bags home with him each day and placed them in the locker of his wardrobe, so that his wife and children did not get to know. To tell the truth, they actually did. They were seriously considering taking Shyamalendu to a psychiatrist when, one sad morning, Hritwik lost control over him. Shyamalendu seemed to have developed a mind of his own. He refused to listen to Hritwik. Shyamalendu planted his feet firmly in the centre of the lushly carpeted floor of his impeccably clean cabin and stayed put. Slowly, silently, surely, he refused to collect the ash from the crystal ash-tray. When Hritwik nibbled his pen and insisted that he pick it up, Shyamalendu, brownpaper bag in hand, giggled like a child, stuck out a thumb at his mentor, blew into the brownpaper bag till it rounded and swelled up like a balloon. Then, as suddenly, he slapped one hand on one side of the bag. It collapsed with a loud *phut*. The ash in the ashtray spilled all over, floated in the air like dots of dust polluting the clinical cleanliness of the airconditioned room. This sudden *volte face* in one of his favourite characters took Hritwik so much by surprise that he stopped nibbling the wrong end of his pen. Slowly, as reality dawned, he discovered that his jaw was open and that his pen had drawn doodles on the page where Shyamalendu was left holding the flattened bag in his hands, shaking his head vigorously thiswayandthat, to point out that he had no immediate plans of budging from where he was. Nor was he interested in collecting ash anymore. What happened to Hritwik's story was, of course, none of his concern.

Ridhhima, another creation of Hritwik's highly imaginative pen, from the story *The Woman who Wanted to be a Fairy* had a different story to tell. Hritwik had christened her with the unusual name in the faint hope that this might just allow him to sustain control over her life, at least, till he finished the story. Riddhima was attractive in a dusky sort of way. She wore ethnic clothes and ornate jewellery crafted out of oxidised silver. Always. A longish, vertical ornamental dot that almost divided her forehead into two and a little lipstick were the only concessions she made to 'makeup'. Always. She had a low, husky voice and threw her lines in a patiently acquired drawl. Always. In sum, she was the living personification of what usually goes for 'sexy chic' in ethnic terms.

Riddhima was married, with a ten-year-old boy. She worked in a bank. Her husband Sanjeeb was a lecturer in Economics at a neighbouring college. Theirs was a love marriage, resulting in both sets of parents having boycotted them till Jojo was born. The once feverishly, violently passionate marriage had matured, mellowed, cooled off and then settled into deep freeze because Sanjeeb had suddenly become sexually impotent. "Must be out of watching all those porn films on video at night," mused Riddhima to herself. But he refused to admit this failure. So psychological or medical counselling was ruled out. Sanjeeb had a bit of a name as a contemporary poet. This added to his shying away from an investigation. In the typical chauvinist's manner of defying a problem by denying it, he refused to acknowledge that there was, at all, a problem. Riddhima was surprised. Sanjeeb was of a quiet, adjusting nature. He was full of consideration for a wife with the dual responsibility of running a home on top of a job and put in his bit as much as he could. Which was quite a bit because his working hours at the college were lesser than Riddhima's at the bank. He always gave in first when and if they had a tiff. It did not take him a second to say 'sorry'.

And the aggressive Riddhima had the last word in the running of the family. That left Sanjeeb to follow his pet passion—composing poetry.

As if with a vengeance, the sex-starved Riddhima slowly, steadily, created a dream-world of her own. In this dream, she turned into a winged fairy to enter into the bedrooms of male filmstars like Salman Khan, Aamir Khan and Shahrukh Khan and made love to them. Their wives did not know because Riddhima made herself invisible. The husbands thought they were actually making love to their wives because for them, Riddhima disguised herself as the wife when she made love. The day she thought of stepping into the bachelor bedroom of the young Hrithik Roshan, the current craze, Shyamalendu, from Hritwik's earlier story, caught her in the act. Hritwik was stumped! "How did Shyamalendu get into the Riddhima story?" he asked himself. "What are *you* doing here?" he barked at Shyamalendu. "Aren't you supposed to be in that other story of mine, picking ash from the ash-tray in your office?" he asked. Shyamalendu did not even acknowledge his presence. He pretended Hritwik did not exist. He carried a pair of scissors with him. In front of Hritwik's shocked eyes, he clipped the pair of wings off Riddhima's shoulders, placed them in one of his stock of brownpaper bags he took out of his pocket and asked her to go home! As if like magic, the beautiful pair of sequinned wings neatly folded themselves into tiny little balls to fit into the small brownpaper bag. He then turned around to face Hritwik, still nibbling his pen and doodling all over the page, to tell him "mind your own business, Mr. Author, and let me mind mine." Riddhima was mesmerised by Shyamalendu. Like an obedient child, she held his hand and began to walk back in the direction of her home.

Hritwik was disgusted. More with himself than with the defiant and rebellious characters he had created. Prabhakar, the teenaged runaway from one of his exciting stories dealing with the disturbed phase of adolescence called *The Teenager*, came back one fine morning, bringing back large smiles on his parents' faces but leaving his creator to wring his tired hands in utter despair. "I was missing my parents badly," he told Hritwik in no uncertain terms. "Besides, it suddenly struck me that leaving them for a flimsy reason like wanting to make it in Hindi films was crazy. I had to live off roasted groundnuts and sleep on the dirty bench of a railway platform. My bed at home is wonderful. So is my maa's cooking. Who are you to decide that I should stay missing? Have you tried going missing yourself as a young boy?" he asked Hritwik, then shrugged, pursed his lips in dismissal and turned in to enjoy a home-cooked dinner with his parents. And who, do you think his mother was? None other than Riddhima, the young lady who hid her fairy wings in the drawer of her kitchen cabinet! Hritwik discovered with shock that Shyamalendu and not Sanjeeb, was Prabhakar's father!

Payal, from the story *Split* who, Hritwik had decided, would walk out of her home and a good husband in the opening sentence of his story was another rebel. Hritwik planned that Payal would leave Gautam because he "was just too good" and because "too-much-of-a-good-thing" can become a bit sickening and dull. But Payal refused to leave Gautam, much less, divorce him. "What do you mean beginning a story with my divorce?" she asked Hritwik angrily.

"If you begin the story with my divorce, what happens to the rest of my life? I don't want to be independent you fool. I love depending on Gautam. I can never imagine leaving him. He's a gem of a husband." Having delivered one of the briefest of speeches in the history of short fiction, Payal went back into the kitchen to finish the chicken pulao she was making for Gautam. Gautam turned around to wink naughtily at Hritwik. "Don't tell her but I am actually having an affair with Shyamalendu's teenaged daughter," he said in an aside, covering his mouth with the back of his hand as he spoke in a whisper. Then, he sat back to enjoy the wonderful aroma of chicken pulao wafting in from the kitchen.

Sanjay, from the short story *Scam*, was a strapping young man who was unwittingly involved in a scam in the bank where he worked as an executive. He was supposed to commit suicide by hanging himself from the ceiling. Hritwik had decided that the shirt he would choose to hang himself from would tear off at the last minute and save him from an ignominious final exit. Sanjay stubbornly turned away from the scam. Hritwik was about to tear off his hair in frustration. Sanjay agreed to commit suicide though, because Reema, his girlfriend, had just broken off with him and decided to marry his best friend Ranjit. But he staunchly refused to be saved from his suicidal act. "I have been successful in everything I have done throughout my short life. How dare you decide that my suicide should end in failure?" he asked Hritwik angrily. Then added in an afterthought, "I wear Blue Diamond shirts, the most expensive and classy shirts in the market. They do not tear even if you hang off them from the top storey of the Empire State Building. Got that?" Having said this, Sanjay proceeded to hang himself from the ceiling fan of his empty flat while Hritwik turned his face away to the potted plant at the foot of his writing table. He could not bear sad scenes.

Hritwik had written not less than twenty short stories, one play and two novels, all within the short span of ten years since his graduation. All of them were in different stages of completion because the characters had run away to make their own lives different from the ones Hritwik had planned for them. He discussed these stories only with his longtime sweetheart, Nilanjana, who was more interested in Hritwik's wonderful job at the ad agency than in his literary experiments. Yet, she listened patiently, encouraged him with soothing words of consolation, but could do nothing to resolve his problem.

Then, something happened to change the course of Hritwik's abortive career in creative fiction. One evening, he came back from work to receive the shocking news of his father's death in a street accident. His parents led a retired life in Pune. As their only child, he had to rush for the last rites. He doubted whether his mother would be able to bear the tragedy, because his parents had shared a close, warm and long married life. Hritwik had resisted all their attempts to get him married off to a girl of their choice. Yet, he was scared to tell them of his decision to marry Nilanjana because she was from a different caste and his parents were caste-conscious. But Nilanjana came along nevertheless. He was happy that she did because her soft presence by his side cushioned the sharp, knife-like edge of pain a little. The rhythmic beat of the train kept time with his journey into his past, a childhood spent with his parents in different parts of the country. As he looked out of the window at the picturesque beauty of the Khandala ghats, his eyes could only see the face of his smiling father as he grew slowly and lovingly from thirty-odd, as Hritwik remembered him first, till a well-lived 75, when he passed away, uncharacteristically, without notice. "It is usage and not age, that is important," his father would say. "Don't use vocabulary that goes against yourself," he would add. From a strapping, slim, young, bespectacled father with thick black hair that he preferred to part down the middle, Hritwik's professor father grew into a soft and podgy-figured man whose vision went from bad to worse, changing the frame and thickness of his glasses and thereby, the way he looked. The thick head of hair began to recede till there was not much left of it except an occasional strand peeping from behind a shining pate. His style of dress, his body language, altered visibly. From neatly tailored three-piece suits, he moved on to kurta-trousers then to dhoti-shirts and then to the humble kurta thrown over a silken lungi. What did not change was his quiet, non-interfering nature, his passion for reading, and his love for his pupils. After many years, Hritwik felt like smoking a cigarette. He fumbled into his pocket and realised he had given up smoking ages ago. His glasses turned misty with tears he was scared to shed. He knew he resembled his father. But only in looks. In temperament, mood, likes and dislikes, he guessed he was more like his mother. Or maybe, like himself. The three-hour train journey seemed to span days instead of hours. The journey towards Pune for Hritwik, turned into an inner journey into a nostalgic past filled with fun and games, love—always understated, and anger—always overstated. Nilanjana remained silent all along, respecting the privacy and loneliness of his grief.

As Hritwik entered a home filled with neighbours and relatives he had long forgotten, and hordes of pupils his father had once taught, now professors themselves, or executives in their shining armour of suits, one film star who had lost his gloss, his mother stepped out to receive them. She wore the mandatory white saree symbolising Hindu widowhood. Her forehead was devoid of the 25p coin-sized red circle that brought a glow to her face, reflecting the strong presence of his father. Yet, she wasn't crying. She wore a tired, sad smile as she welcomed the two of them into the house. "He made me promise I'd never cry," she whispered softly, with a catch in her throat, as together, they crossed the threshold. He looked at her. But she had turned her face away by then. For the first time, he recognised in her, a strength he did not believe she had.

Among the people that had gathered, he was surprised to spot his Shyamalendu and his Riddhima and Prabhakar and Payal and Sanjay. They furrowed their brows and frowned at him in anger. They pointed their accusing forefinger at him for playing with their lives against their wishes. They floated around as phantomly and ethereal figures superimposed against the concrete real people around. As his mother personally went around offering her visitors lemon juice from crystal-clear tall glasses she had saved up for his marriage, Hritwik realised that no one else could see the characters born out of the private island of his literary dreams. He watched as his mother walked through Shyamalendu to offer a glass of juice to a lady sitting behind where Shyamalendu stood. An uncle from the past he could not recognise came up to pat his back in consolation. Riddhima, watching from behind, smirked at his slight embarassment. He was still numb from the shock of the sudden loss of a father he loved deeply. Slowly, very slowly, the grief was beginning to soak into him. This strange blend of his characters with his grief was confusing for Hritwik. He resolved the confusion somewhat, with glances thrown back again and again at his mother who defined grief in a way distanced from his common sense expectations of how it ought to be expressed.

Soft sounds of a woman's sobbing overlapped whispered exchanges among the not-too-small crowd. Death was too real. No woman could sprout wings even if she was created from the figment of his imagination. If you invested a character with a strange eccentricity, you needed to explain it somewhere along the way. If a teenager ran away from home, he always could be expected to come back. In a social ambience where women were forced to stay back even when they had enough reason to walk out, a woman like Payal would never walk out of an excellent husband like Gautam. A man as successful and as brilliant as Sanjay would never take the easy way out by committing suicide. Or, even if he did, he would find ways more devious and sophisticated than hanging off a ceiling fan with the help of a shirt. Perhaps, Hritwik's characters were too much of fantasy and had too little of the real. Perhaps, his sense of the real was overshadowed by his fondness for fantasy. Perhaps, that is why he could not finish his stories.

It turned out to be the most grindingly slow day of his entire life. Crawling minutes seemed to drag and drag and drag into long, long hours mapping the landscape of his mind with memories of a happy mother trading jokes with his father. Memories of that lovingly tended rose garden in Kanpur, where his father was posted for a while, and Hritwik was at school. Memories of walking along a moonlit beach at Puri where they had holidayed after Hritwik finished his school's final exams. Memories of watching the kite festival in Ahmedabad when Hritwik was in a college hostel and had come visiting for the vacations. Watching, fascinated, with his arm around his father's shoulder, the January sky playing hide-and-seek with coloured triangles, squares, rectangles and diamonds of kites, kites and more kites.

Visitors mouthed words of sympathy, some real, some simulated, some plastic. Most of them left soon after the rituals were over. A few stayed behind to help. At last, he readied himself to sit down to lunch with his mother, her old maid and Nilanjana, who, by then, had made herself comfortable in the kitchen. The heady smell of burning incense blending into the fragrance of white circular rings of nightqueen flowers was a bit too strong on nerves already weakened with the razor-sharp silence of loss. He shared with his mother, a spartan lunch of rice and dal cooked on an earthen pot over an instant earthen oven, eaten with a dash of rock salt, as was the Bengali custom. Then, he saw her shed a few tears. They seemed to flow freely and without warning, blending into the rice. She mixed the tears quickly into the rice-dal mixture, hoping Hritwik would not notice. He did. He shed some too, surprised as this sudden visible expression of his feelings for his grieving mother. The food tasted a bit more salty for his taste. Whether it was due to those tears, he did not know. He decided that if he really had to finish a story, he would have to rid himself of indulging in fantasy.

When all the guests had left in the evening, and his mother had retired for the night, lying on a blanket-covered bed of hay, Hritwik walked into his old study and opened his wardrobe. The room was clean, but for a thin layer of dust that had gathered on the furniture and a soft musty smell because it was opened only when he came down. Among clothes he never wore now, on one of the shelves, he counted the small brownpaper bags he had collected as a student when he smoked like a chimney. Though he had given up smoking long ago, the ash of those days was neatly collected and poured into brownpaper bags to be stored and saved for a story he could not finish. Among the uniformed row of brownpaper bags, stood a slightly larger one. He opened it gingerly because it was cracking up a bit. He peeped inside. He found what he was looking for—a pair of fairy wings he had stolen as a boy when his school had staged a fairy play and the wings had gone missing, never to be found. The girl playing the fairy had to make do without them. He took out an old, single-lined, hardcover notebook, closed the wardrobe shut, and turned back to sit on his old desk. He switched on the table lamp, picked an old fountain pen from the pen stand, wiped the dust with the hem of his kurta, then opened the forgotten notebook he had bought many years ago to begin his writing career in. The call from Mumbai had beckoned with a job he could not refuse. So, none of the pages could get written into. He avoided looking at the wall in front, afraid of seeing 'their' shadows perform a ghostly dance in the dim light of the table lamp. He did not want them to tease or mock him anymore. He shut his ears to their imagined whispers, mocking him, teasing him, challenging him to make them real and to complete each story. He closed his nose to shut out the musty smell of dust. Then, in his calligraphic handwriting, he composed the first line of his new story...

*"The problem with Hritwik was that he could never finish any story that he began...*